That Great Big Trenchcoat in the Sky

That Great Big Trenchcoat in the Sky

MARC LOVELL

PUBLISHED FOR THE CRIME CLUB BY

Doubleday ⚓ **New York**
1988

Library of Congress Cataloging-in-Publication Data
Lovell, Marc.
That great big trenchcoat in the sky.
(Crime club)
I. Title.
PR6062.0853T45 1988   823'.914   87-19642
ISBN 0-385-24316-2

That Great Big Trenchcoat in the Sky

ONE

Being nervous, Apple drove like a beginner, all spurt and veer, dawdle and weave. His hands gripped the steering-wheel as fervently as he was holding in thought to the source of his nervousness: what lay ahead on this mild autumn evening. His features were set in a grim pose.

Appleton Porter was a pale man who generally wore a pale expression, as though the showing of strong feelings had to be avoided in the name of decency. It was not out of choice. He would have loved to display firing-squad sneers or those bent smiles of the blasé, in the same way that he would have been thrilled to dress more adventurously than in his undertaker suits and banker ties; but, he felt, passionate expressions no more went with freckles and neat gingery hair than exotic dress went with respectable philologists. Apple had a fierce sense of what was right, in all directions, which depressed him only some of the time.

Dusk had been approaching slowly since Apple had crossed the river at Blackfriars Bridge. Now, lamps came glumly alive along the kerbs of inner suburbia, changing the streets from misty enigmas to celebrations of the drab.

Apple put his lights on. This area of south-east London was fairly unknown to him, which added to his tension, fueled his doubts. Like all sincere neurotics, Apple was happiest with the familiar.

His feelings he forgot on turning into yet another quiet, tepid street. Seeing a group of children at play under a lamp and half in the roadway, he slowed for safety. Pleasure took him as every child without exception halted play to stare at Ethel.

In odd poses like saggy scarecrows the group watched her bowl elegantly by, and when she was leaving them behind, they raised a ragged cheer.

The spontaneity warmed Apple further. His faint, almost reverent smile lasted until he rounded a bend and realised he was getting closer.

Part consolation for Apple in respect of clothing, Ethel was painted a variety of screaming colours. Where these might have looked merely tinkly on a modern car, they struck gleeful chimes on a vehicle that was not only more than thirty years old but was unmistakably a tall, square London taxi, complete with hire sign on the roof.

In truth, however, Ethel had never roamed the Big Smoke's byways looking for trade, nor waited in orderly ranks, nor been used as a brothel on wheels, nor hidden whenever it rained. She had gone straight into undercover work, initially police, ultimately the Intelligence services. Apple had become her owner when she had been retired and brutally sent to suffer the auctioneer's hammer.

Ethel, in fact, formed Appleton Porter's strongest connexion with the world of espionage, though he continued to believe that his love and pride stemmed from her being the finery which his shyness wouldn't allow him to wear. Apple preferred to think of himself as a failed flamboyant rather than an admitted romantic.

For romantic, mainly, was how Apple saw the espionage business, in which he served as an underling, like a lowly clerk in a department store. He had read more spy novels than he had met spies. He knew more about Mata

Hari than he did about Angus Watkin, his Control. He envisioned the headquarters of his particular department, known as Upstairs, which he had never been invited to visit, as a cross between a palace and a luxury penthouse—yet wouldn't have minded learning that it was a scruffiness hiding far underground beneath Victoria Station, for that too was romantic.

Apple had experienced little of the cynicism, sick violence and treachery that were constants in the spy game, perhaps the only game in which a winner might be the one who broke the most rules. On those rare occasions when Angus Watkin had sent him out into the field as an agent, he had never been thoroughly disillusioned, only bemused or disappointed, between being plumply satisfied.

There were several reasons Apple wasn't used more frequently, beginning with his height. At six feet seven inches it took immense ingenuity to make yourself blend with the crowd; and Apple was not ingenious.

However, he did manage to turn his tiresome height into the sole scapegoat, the one fault that held him back in his career as a special agent, thus reducing his other drawbacks to mere trifles. He wasn't totally naive, this Apple, at least not in respect to himself.

Peering ahead on the dim-lit street, its row houses as lovely as flies on a baby's face, Apple looked out for the nameplate of Meen Lane. When he saw it, he twitched with nerves. In changing gear, preparing to slow and make the turn, he created a grind in Ethel's transmission.

All at the same time, Apple gritted his teeth, tightly closed one eye and shot up his shoulders like the last Gallic shrug. That over with and the dashboard patted in apology, he released a soggy string of scatological words. Not one of them would have been understood by anybody who knew only English, who had none of the seventeen foreign languages Apple drew on. Also, he whispered.

Appleton Porter, senior official at the United Kingdom Philological Institute, a real job as well as cover, did have a certain value to Upstairs as a translator/interpreter. He sat in on international conferences between spymasters, wrote letters of love or extortion, checked decoded transcripts, listened to taped conversations to judge if a speaker's language was original or acquired.

As Apple knew, there were many like himself attached to the armed but silent forces, in any country. They were the faceless ones. Like eager but limited actors they were called on once in a while to perform, accept a crumb. Their speciality might be archery, lipreading, safe-cracking, walking a tightrope or even the ability to sweat at will.

Often Apple reminded himself of how lucky he was. He had at least actually been used on missions as an operative, whereas your average faceless one simply came onstage, did his party piece, left without getting any applause and went back to obscurity for another year or two or five.

The reminder helped make even more trifling for Apple those drawbacks that were inscribed in his Upstairs dossier, at goodly length, as though, like gossip, the foul was far more fun than the fair.

Porter was an infomaniac. "People who collect esoteric and useless data tend to be disinterested in facts of value or immediacy, therefore poor both at pursuit and retention of same."

Porter was sentimental. "People who respond to their feelings were liable to respond to the feelings of others, which can lead to negative emotions such as compassion, understanding, affection and, in extreme cases, love."

Porter had a fervent dislike of weapons, guns in particular. "No comment."

Porter had scored the lowest marks in his squad during training (apart from Security Rating and Languages), being especially dismal in Lying, Acting Ability, Unarmed Combat, Tolerance for Alcohol, Resistance to Pain. "No comment."

The dossier concluded that Appleton Porter did not have the makings of an undercover agent, even without taking into account his final, outstanding drawback.

Meen Lane bore left. Apple, who had been noting house numbers, slowed as he took the curve. He was flexing one arm in a try at bravado.

On the right loomed a ponderous building. Dark, cheery as a dead cat, it could have been a warehouse or a workhouse or a riff-raff whorehouse.

Passing, Apple found an empty slot among the vehicles lined up at the kerbs. Parking, he locked Ethel carefully and threw a warning glance around at the shadowy desertion before going back to the bulky building.

A short flight of steps led Apple down into further dimness, to a door which bore scabby paint and the right number. After knocking firmly, he was seized with the urge to run. He stared in panic at the door.

It opened. The woman who looked out at him from the feebly lit passage was in her early twenties. She had straight fair hair to the shoulders and a solemn but attractive face. Her sweater, skirt and shoes were dark, plain and sensible. She made Apple think of an escaped nun.

He said, "I'm Appleton Porter."

"We talked on the telephone," the girl said. "I'm Jennifer Rolph." She drew the door wider. "Welcome to Blushers Anonymous."

Meen Hall (hirable by the hour, Apple learned) was a stark basement of two hundred disorganized chairs, the smell of decaying umbrellas, a platform raised far enough from floor level to trip over and the inevitable tea-urn in a corner which, aided by a dangle of curtain, was pretending to be an alcove.

Twelve to fifteen people were gathered near the tea corner, some standing, some squeakily on the folding seats. The youngest person was a boy in his gawky teens, all hands and Adam's apple, the oldest a woman of sixty-odd, all perk and verve.

Lady Barre, widow of Sir Jack Barre, who had failed to climb all the world's tallest mountains, or so she told Apple on introduction, apropos of nothing, was stout to a degree that packed tight her bib-overalls of bright red velveteen. Her face was matchingly round and pink and youthful, with an active mouth and surprised eyes. The hanks of grey hair that straggled down from her untidy topknot she flicked up between gestures or blew up between words.

Lady Barre was the founder of Blushers Anonymous. This Apple learned from Jennifer Rolph ("Call me Jen"), who sat beside him on a row jotting down his particulars in a school exercise book.

"Does she always dress like that?"

Jennifer said, "Well, she has in the two months since I've been her driver-secretary-companion. Except that her overalls are usually blue or green. She wears red to Blushers Anonymous meetings by way of compensation."

They were speaking quietly, as were several others, while Lady Barre stood by the tea-urn talking at those nearby. Apple asked, "You mean to compensate for the fact that she's not a blusher herself?"

"Precisely, Appleton," Jennifer Rolph said, giving him

a quick upward glance. She had green eyes. Apple liked green eyes. He himself had green eyes.

"How about you, Jen?"

"Oh, I blush, of course, as most people do, but it's not the morbid condition of the afflicted."

"You're lucky."

"Which means, I take it, that you are not."

Apple nodded. He was not. Hot flushes had been the curse of his life and a large drawback in his secret career. He had tried dozens of so-called cures, as well as acupuncture and a lotion that was supposed to keep the face a permanent pink (it mottled).

When, some days ago, Apple had seen the small item in a newspaper's personal column, announcing the existence of Blushers Anonymous, he had been delighted but skeptical. Bravely he had dialled the number, tensely he had come, cautiously he stayed.

"These personal details are in the strictest confidence, by the by," Jennifer Rolph said, closing her book. "Even members' last names aren't known to anyone except Lady Barre and myself."

"Does that help?"

"It seems to."

"Then I'm all for it."

"Now if you'll excuse me," Jennifer said in her neat, formal way. Rising, she went to the two people who had arrived after Apple, who noted that she had decent calves.

Presently the comforting murmur of voices was sliced by a resonant call for attention. It came from Lady Barre. She was standing on tip-toe, arms raised as if about to conduct the silence that had fallen like a shot horse.

Clicking on a smile, Lady Barre said in a throb, "Welcome, old and new members, sufferers all, to this our third meeting of Blushers Anonymous. I harbour hopes that my brainchild will produce concrete results. I want you all to look forward with confidence to cures or vast improvements. Mmm?"

The group mumbled, shuffled, sniffed. Lady Barre said with a wink, "You're all going to be as white as chalk." Like an amateur comic, she laughed at her own joke.

The group stayed silent, unamused.

Feeling sorry for the speaker, Apple laughed. Slowly, everyone turned to look at him. He tensed. With horror, he sensed the approach of a blush.

There was nothing he could do. He was too furious to try out the latest short-term cure, sent to him by an afflicted cousin who worked in an Australian nudist colony. It entailed picturing yourself in a rocket, closing in on the sun. The imagined heat would kill your blush, claimed the cousin, if it was no stronger than a grade three.

Peering with anxious eyes, Lady Barre asked, "Is something wrong, Appleton?"

If she didn't understand, most everyone else did, as, with sick smile and eyes suggesting tragedy, Apple produced on his face a redness as thorough and lush as diaper-rash. The response from the knowing was standard: diversion.

The people burst into talk. Looking everywhere but at the victim of their carelessness, they tossed out loud comments on subjects such as earwigs, bee-keeping and holidays in Belfast.

Since, evidently, some of the subjects found favour, individual talk swiftly changed to pockets of natural conversation. Cooling gratefully, Apple acknowledged not for the first time that blushers were inclined to be eccentric. He was glad he was different.

Some time passed before peace returned, what with

the late couple arguing about tree-pruning and Lady Barre getting involved in a debate on frozen food.

During this time Apple established eye contact with a girl he hadn't noticed before. Mid to late twenties, features strong and dark, hair cut like a wealthy urchin, she looked fetchingly mysterious in a black raincoat.

She had smiled sympathetically at Apple, who had given back a smile of thanks. Thereafter, whenever their eyes met (the girl wasn't conversing), diffident smiles followed. Apple, sitting small, was intrigued.

Jennifer Rolph brought peace by reminding everyone that time was in limited supply, others would be needing the hall soon.

"Ah yes, those poor unknown drunks," Lady Barre said. She took up her position again and began to talk of Aims.

The hope was that sufferers of the blushing malady would benefit from meeting their own kind, Apple gathered; from exchanging ideas on how to combat attacks; from investigating the possibility of diet being efficacious; from reading the latest findings on the matter by psychiatrists; from giving each other moral support.

"Another important point," Lady Barre said, blowing a hank of hair aside, "is that we do what we may never have had the valour to do before—stand up in front of other people and talk. Without, of course, suffering an attack."

There was a general clearing of throats, as if someone had asked for money. Apple glanced at the dark girl. She looked preoccupied.

"Last time that was quite jolly," Lady Barre said with a preen up on her toes. "Right?"

People mumbled while looking at the floor. "Right," Lady Barre agreed. "So we'll go on with that now. Whose turn is it, Jen?"

Jennifer read out from her notebook, "Norman."

Swaying like a schoolboy picked on to recite, a middle-aged man got up and went to take the founder's place as she moved aside. He carried a newspaper. Once in position facing the group, he opened his paper and with both hands held it in front of his face. There was nothing to be seen of the man but fingers and lower body.

"Yes," Lady Barre said, making the word last two seconds. "Well, it's a start. In a manner of speaking. Rome wasn't built in a week, and so forth."

Jennifer Rolph said, "Questions, please."

Lady Barre, gazing around brightly: "I know we all have lots of questions for Norman, haven't we?"

It took more coaxing before the members obliged, initially in timid whispers. With the newspaper trembling slightly like on Monday morning, Norman told of the type of work he did, his current marriage, the first and last time he had blushed, what he did for it, how often it happened when he was alone and the reason he felt Blushers Anonymous could be useful.

When, to polite clapping, Norman had folded his paper and returned to his chair, Lady Barre asked for another name. The woman who answered Jennifer's summons got only three steps from her seat before going quickly back to it. Apple cringed for her and Jennifer called out, "Wendy."

It was the dark girl. She got up as promptly as a prize-winner, went toward the tabled tea-urn and at the last moment slipped behind the curtain. Unseen, she said, "Ready."

After giving another of her two-second yeses, Lady Barre asked, "How long have you been a sufferer, dear?"

"Since I was fifteen," Wendy said. With encouragement she went on to tell of disputing angrily with a queue-jumper in a shop, of winning, of then being unable to remember what she wanted. "It all started there."

Someone asked, "Do you blush when you're alone?"

"Oh yes," the ghostly voice said. "Frequently. I don't want to go into details, but for one thing I always undress with the light out."

Among sympathetic murmurs Norman said, "Sounds like a severe affliction to me."

Apple agreed. He further agreed with himself when he pointed out mentally that, if nothing else, this kind of thing made Blushers Anonymous worthwhile: the knowledge that there was always someone worse off than yourself.

Sitting taller he asked, "Wendy, what's your job?"

"No particulars, please," interrupted Jennifer Rolph. "Just state the type."

From behind the curtain came, "I can't tell about it anyway. My work's what they call 'sensitive,' although actually it's nothing special."

A woman asked, "Have you ever been married?"

"Heavens, no. I've never even had a really steady boy friend, only casuals."

"Are they usually blushers, or decidedly otherwise?"

There came another interruption. This time it was from the mouth of the entry passage, a raucous coughing produced by a man with a collarless shirt. Cough ended, he said, "You got five minutes left."

The passage was the scene of a minor panic. Chatting and laughing like the audience leaving a boring play, ordeal over, the members of Blushers Anonymous thronged exitward at different speeds, from hasty to dawdle, while at the same time people with dry mouths and martyr eyes moved in the opposite direction.

Wading, Apple finally caught up. He said a casual, "Hello there. I'm Appleton."

Wendy smiled. "Hi. You asked about work. I recognise the voice." She was tall for a woman, about five-eight by Apple's appreciative reckoning, though he knew that he was apt to add an inch or so if he took a true fancy to a girl. Which meant, he realised, that he had taken a fancy here because he knew, his eye being infallible in matters of height, that Wendy was definitely five feet seven and a quarter inches tall.

He asked, "Is this your first time?"

"Second. I don't know if it'll do any good but I'm going to give it a whirl."

"My feelings exactly."

"I think it's a great idea, though. Somebody ought to give Lady B a medal. She's really something."

"Is she well known?"

Wendy said, "Last year, I hear, she was campaigning for dog shows to be banned, claiming they were degrading for the animals. Before that she was into prison reform."

Apple, who had been taking more notice of Wendy's lips than of the words they were offering, said, "My car's nearby. Maybe I could give you a lift home."

"I don't mind a walk."

"It's a bit crummy, this area, especially at night."

"Not really. I live here."

Gasping a laugh: "What I meant was . . ."

"In fact," Wendy said, "if I hadn't been a few streets away I don't know if I would have come to BA. Frankly, I think I'm terribly brave."

"Oh, you are, you are," Apple said in that grovelling way of his that he didn't mind now but would remember with disgust when he was cleaning his teeth.

"You're brave as well, Appleton. We all are."

A hand from behind grabbed Apple's arm. Slowing, he turned. It was one of the members, a man called Jasper. He had asked most of the questions, which suited his prosecutor appearance. Fifty-odd, tallish and girder straight, clothing as immaculate as a tailor's conception, he had a hawk-nosed face under hair that was as dense and white as the wigs of court. The spectacles he stared through were square, like twin Judas-holes.

"It's Appleton, right?" he asked, solemn.

Apple nodded while trying to free his arm without seeming to be doing so and turning back toward Wendy in order to keep the contact alive. She was moving ahead.

Dragging like an anchor, Jasper said, "Look here, Appleton, I owe you an apology. It was brutal of me to gape at you when you laughed."

"Everyone did. Natural response. No problem."

"I do, nevertheless, apologise."

"Accepted," Apple said out of the side of his mouth while waving for attention at Wendy, who, in profile, was talking to another member as they moved smoothly along the passage.

Jasper: "Decent of you."

"Not at all."

"To be honest, I'm surprised at myself, as well as shocked."

"Good," Apple said absently as he managed to wrench his arm free of Jasper's prosecutor grip. But now the human stream had clogged. In front of him were several of the new arrivals, causing him to slow still more. Only violence would have given him clearance. He sighed.

"The thing is, I should have known better," Jasper said doggedly. "I live with that kind of thing every day."

"So do we all."

"Not in quite the same way. You see, I'm here under false pretences."

Apple looked at him. "Oh?"

"I myself am not a blusher. It's my wife who has the problem. And believe me, a problem it has been."

"You can't have had it easy."

With an invalid weave of his head Jasper said, "No, by God. But I did learn to live with it in time. One adapts." He went on telling of his hard travail as they moved along the passage, Apple restlessly. Wendy was no longer in sight among the cram of heads.

Nor was she to be seen on the glum-lit street when finally Apple gained the outdoors. He would have sighed again except for telling himself not to fret, there was another meeting in two days. He set off along the street, at which stage he realised he still had the company of Jasper, who was still talking as if he hated to see the jury leave.

"Well, good night," Apple said, proud of his cruelty.

"As long as you understand."

"Absolutely. Sleep well."

"She's a bit on the shy side, the little woman, so I thought I'd come in her place. I thought I might pick up something she could use."

Apple made appropriate sounds to that and the following comments until they stopped by Ethel, when Jasper snorted, "Look at that bloody mess."

Apple creaked himself rigid. He asked an aghast, "What did you say?"

"This beautiful old car. Look what some idiot's done to it."

"This beautiful old car, sir, is mine."

Unfazed, Jasper said forgivingly that some people had odd ideas when they got in the carnival spirit. "And this new wash-off paint is quite harmless, I understand."

Holding to the fact that the oaf had, after all, called Ethel beautiful, Apple merely grunted. The oaf said, "You are, naturally, a member of ALTOG."

Two minutes later, driving away, Apple thought about the Antique London Taxicab Owners Guild. He had been aware of it for years. It was one of the lesser-known associations, small and select. Its name wasn't bandied about. People spoke it with heavy eyelids. Occasionally you might see a man wearing the ALTOG tie—black with a broken white line down the middle.

Last year Ethel had become eligible to join, having reached the right age. Apple had done nothing. Now, however, he pondered the matter. After all, he thought, he had joined Blushers Anonymous, which had led to a mention of ALTOG, so maybe that was a sign that he should act. Certainly it was time he got over thinking that just because Ethel was an antique that didn't make her an old crone.

While musing thus Apple had been conscious in another part of his mind of a pair of headlights; the same pair that had been behind him ever since he had left Meen Lane. A distinguishing feature was a yellowness of one of the lights.

Apple left ALTOG in favour of the present when after rounding a bend he saw that the car was still there, lying some fifty yards back.

He was half pleased, half embarrassed. He liked the intrigue but knew it was probably false, for in order to keep in practice he often played the tailing game. Either he pretended he was being followed or he chose a car to stay behind, to tail as inobtrusively as he could.

Apple put on speed. Ethel swept fussily along the quiet street, a lady being bothered by a masher. Via his rear-view mirror, Apple saw the ill-matched eyes come on again after an initial pause.

What he didn't see was the car itself. It stayed merely a hint of gleams behind the brightness of its headlights, what with the streetlamps hereabouts being dull, as though the lower orders had higher vision.

With acutely less embarrassment now Apple headed for the nearest main thoroughfare, where the lighting would be so stark you could read a palm by it. He didn't waste his time on speculation about the person behind, although he did hope it wasn't one of those fools who follow you because they want to play Cops and Robbers or something.

After half a dozen twists through the unlovely streets, Apple came to a thruway, grim but efficient, straight as an arthritic pickpocket and bright as a midway.

He drove along it at a sedate thirty. The headlights did not appear behind. He slowed. In the rear distance, the odd eyes came from around the turning. He stopped and twisted around to get a clearer sighting than in the mirror. But the vehicle was too far back for him to see anything other than it seemed to be a private car, size average. Even colour was doubtful.

The car also stopped. Apple's hesitation was brief. He slotted first gear in, let a bus go by, then zoomed into a fast curve. As soon as he was around facing the other way he saw that the mystery car was reversing back into the side street.

Apple poured on the power. Ethel shuddered like an outraged dowager, but responded well, slicking along at speed under the glare as though happy to show what she could do.

It wasn't enough. When Apple cut off into the side street he saw desertion. The mystery car, no doubt young, had escaped.

Next morning at eleven o'clock Apple walked along an alley on the humbler side of Hampstead. On either hand were the walls of back gardens, some high and growing broken glass, some low enough to sit on if it hadn't been for the spikes, some pausing to allow the presence of a garage. The garbage cans gave off a stench that stayed merely a hint for Apple, who, at six seven, tended to be above such things.

He came to a one-car garage whose doors were open. Words on the lintel informed that Stanley Field repaired bicycles. Inside was a mess of frames and wheels, tyres and tubes, greasy rags and boxes of bits. In a centre space stood a man. Like a witch doctor making spells, he was bashing two pieces of metal together while singing gruffly.

Himself fond of sea shanties, Apple was wondering whether or not to interrupt when the man noticed him. He asked, "Well?"

"Am I addressing Mr. Field, the Honourable Secretary of the Antique London Taxicab Owners Guild?"

"That same," the man said. He was close to seventy, wiry as a young terrier, hair pinky white, face as gnarled as a baked walnut. His shirt and corduroys were home to a hundred oil dribbles and spottings. "I admit to everythink." His accent was damp Cockney.

"I telephoned you a while ago, Mr. Field. Appleton Porter. How do you do."

"Come in, mate."

Since he could see no possible route through the mechanical undergrowth, Apple simply shuffled closer in the garage's mouth. He said, "Thank you."

"Be wiv you in a sec," Stanley Field said. He returned to his singing and clanging.

Apple stood in a polite stoop, one which would give

away neither his impatience nor his uncertainty. He still wasn't sure about this.

Never in his life had Apple been a joiner—until last night. What he didn't like about being in, was that it meant others were, of course, out. Yet at the same time he had a need to belong. He sometimes wondered if that was a major reason for his attachment to Upstairs.

Always Apple had kept Ethel free of club entanglements. She had received overtures from the Venerable Vehicle Lovers, Old Crocks Brotherhood, Golden Years Motor Club, Association of Ancient Car Enthusiasts, Senior Automobile Friends. These rivals had painted pretty views of themselves and said bitter things about the others.

They were all fairly decent, Apple supposed, but they were not ALTOG. They were not the top. Just any old body could join them, almost, a golfed-up old Caddy, a danced-out Morris. It was no feather in your luggage-rack to be AACE or SAF. Their membership ran into the thousands where ALTOG, it was rumoured, had only eighty-seven members, including four in North America and one in New Zealand. ALTOG was something else.

Apple had often daydreamed of squelching those classic-car snobs who splurge on about their Jags and their Edsels and their early Minis. He had pictured himself murmuring, "Excuse me. I mustn't be late for my ALTOG meeting."

But the problem was, Apple felt, would joining the association turn him into a snob as well? Would he be gradually corrupted by the power? Would *he* become a splurger on, dropping those magic initials all over the place while grossly fingering the club tie?

Song and clang over, Stanley Field tossed the parts aside and hipped his oil-dark hands. He faced Apple like a headmaster who wasn't about to stand for any non-sense. "Right."

"I'd like to enquire about membership, Mr. Field," Apple said. "I'm considering joining."

Showing dentures of a fierce whiteness, which rendered the smile less sardonic, Field said, "Nice of you. And nice of us if we let you in. It's not often we gets a new member. Every year we turns away hundreds."

"I'm aware of that, Mr. Field."

"See, mate, it's a matter of credentials, that's what it's a matter of."

Apple patted his pockets. "Yes."

"By which I mean the ve-hicle in question as well as her papers. For instance, you might own a clapped-out banger."

"I might but I don't."

"Or again," Stanley Field said, "could be what you've got is a *Glasgow* taxicab. You'd be surprised what some people try on. But we've got experts. You won't got nothink phony past the entry committee, y'know."

"Mr. Field," Apple said, cool. "My vehicle is in excellent condition, has no false parts, is a genuine *London* taxi and is the right age."

The cycle mechanic looked caught between disappointed and skeptical. He asked, almost snapping, "Model and year?"

Apple told him, adding with one eyebrow taut, "She has cantilevered ondrums and the famed Peterson step."

"With twin flanches?"

"Certainly."

"Has she, like my Phyllis, got the wheel-base denks under each gamper?"

With a faint, trenchant smile Apple said, "Denks were discontinued the year before Ethel was made, Mr. Field.

She has the Benz spleen-bearings, as I'm sure you must be aware."

Not at all put out at having his bluff called, Stanley Field said, "My Phyllis has two aptulated fulcrums."

Apple, quickly: "So has Ethel."

"Oh."

"They're quite common, as a matter of fact."

"I wouldn't say that."

"Ethel also has a Bonetti fog-lamp."

The man shrugged, just as though Bonetti fog-lamps were something you came across every day. He said, "My Phyllis is a little too *old* for that kind of modern stuff."

Pretending not to hear this pulling of age rank, which was in the poorest possible taste, Apple said casually, gazing around the workshop meanwhile, "All Ethel's windows are original. Not one has ever been broken."

That he had scored showed in the way Stanley Field did a fast fold of his arms. "Glass," he muttered. "What does a bit of glass matter?"

Relentless, Apple said, "One other little thing Ethel has, Mr. Field, is the celebrated Hammersmith cam-slot with the spliced seg-counter over the first and last pilfers."

As though trying to throw his hands away, Field viciously unfolded his arms. "I'm a very busy man, Mr. Porter," he said, cold as a paradigm for stepfathers.

"So am I, Mr. Field."

"And I would like to remind you that talk's cheap but money buys houses."

"That is so true," Apple said.

"Anyone can *claim* to have this and have that. The proof of the pudding is in the eating."

"I couldn't have put it better myself."

Stanley Field breathed in through his nose. "Call me

when you're ready and I'll give you an appointment to appear before the entry committee. If you show up without your ve-hicle's papers, forget it. Documentation first, next the inspection." He smiled thinly. "Then we'll see what's what, won't we?"

Apple's smile was even thinner. "We certainly will," he said, determined now that Ethel should belong to the Antique London Taxicab Owners Guild. "Good day to you, sir."

"And a good day to *you*, sir."

Apple stopped on the way into Central London to have lunch. He chose a Chinese restaurant so he could find those inevitable mistakes in the menu's Mandarin script and feel clever, feed his ego as well as his belly, though he was aware only of the latter desire.

Spring roll finished, sweet-and-sour pork started, menu devastated, Apple became beset by a couple of thoughts. Niggle One came first but was muffled almost at once by Niggle Two, which was of an entirely different source and nature, chalk-mark to a cheese-knife.

After juggling niggles for a while, conscious dimly that he had been through this last night with the same One and another Two, Apple got up from his food and went to the telephone. He dialled the bicycle repair-shop. He told Stanley Field that he was quite right, aptulated fulcrums were not all that common.

Back at his table, free to tackle Niggle One, Apple was unsurprised when, with little progress made, the hand-holding stage in seduction, his mind ran more interference. He started thinking of the painstaking ablution Ethel was going to get before he presented her to the ALTOG entry committee.

That Apple was unsurprised stemmed from the fact that, in launching himself at One, he had felt a heat growing on his chest from armpit to armpit. Niggle One had the ability to discomfort him. Every time he tried to tackle it, his mind would start protective proceedings with other thoughts.

During the rest of the meal Apple dwelled contentedly on Ethel's ablutions: the toothbrushing of her radiator, the waxing of her leather, the polishing of her windows with newsprint (the ink worked wonders), the lamp-blacking of her rubber, the final wipeover with diesel oil to give her paint that rich, profound, luminous quality.

After lunch Apple penetrated the West End. Ethel he left by a three-hour parking metre near Oxford Street. In another backwater street he entered a building that was as noticeable as a black dog asleep in the dark. The lobby's porter yawned at him from behind his desk.

On an upper floor Apple passed through a door on whose frosted glass it said Bigelow Titles. The vestibule's cubbyhole featured a plain woman who sniffed at him with disapproval, as if he were beautiful, before pressing a buzzer. An inner door opened. Apple passed through.

The grim-furnished conference room had two groups of men, standing one at either end of a long table. Apple joined the four interpreters, ordinary men of the type who retire from behind counters with a watch and a nice pension. The five in the other group were spymasters.

Four of the middle-aged men had undoubted style, from the West German's dark glasses and cheroot to the Turk's satanic beard, from the Norwegian's massive size to the Frenchman's black eye-patch, scarred chin and cigarette-holder. The fifth man was Angus Watkin.

Apple's Control had all the racy style of a shopping list. He was average to an offensive degree. Even his voice lacked colour, like the brown paper lining a damp cupboard. His eyes weren't sharp, his forehead wasn't high.

He looked as though he might aspire to selling no less than two vacuum cleaners a day. Angus Watkin was that man who has lived along the street from you for ever but you've never bothered to wonder about him.

Presently everyone sat down, each interpreter beside and slightly to the rear of his superior. Since the spymasters all spoke several languages, if not with perfection, the talk proceeded in English, French and German, switching easily. The interpreters were used only when matters became serious, such as who was going to pay for what.

The matter these past days had been related to joint training schemes. Apple soon stopped listening, stopped telling himself that here he was, sitting with some of the most powerful spooks in the espionage business. His thoughts drifted to the girl called Wendy.

From there, within seconds, he was thinking Niggle One. He went on. By allowing its absurdity, he found, he was able to avoid emotional discomfort. Smiling whimsically, therefore, Apple considered the notion of Blushers Anonymous being a Communist conspiracy.

See, his mind pointed out, contact is always the big problem in the gathering of information. Recruitment, be it via ideals or payment or fear or extortion, can happen only after a mark has been cultivated; first you have to meet him, and under respectable, rigidly unsuspicious circumstances.

Blushers Anonymous fills the post. The afflicted, like dyslexics, are usually intelligent people and so have the ability to rise to positions of prominence in all fields. The organizers' hope is that they'll isolate a valuable mark occasionally, in particular when their creation, Blushers Anonymous, has spread until there's a chapter in all the world's major cities. Being blushers, therefore sensitive, the marks of value would, in theory, present few problems to those who would manipulate them.

With his smile gone, Apple allowed that the idea was not all that ridiculous. Certainly BA would cost nothing to operate. The one big objection came from its conception, here, for it wasn't likely that Lady Barre was a Communist, though she could be a closet one or a fellow traveller. Could even be that the KGB had forced her into this rôle. Or be paying her handsomely.

Apple shook his head, nodded. He had the ideal solution. It was Good Intentions. Eccentrics like Lady Barre were exactly the kind of innocent do-gooders who got used this way by the secret services of all countries.

In this one, a KGB agent presents himself to the mark as a representative of British Intelligence. He asks her to help in a certain scheme, to serve her country. He makes a thorough job of waving the flag. That part of it is easiest, though it can take hints of medals, honours etc. if the mark's nationalism is feeble. Harder is making her accept that the agent is genuine. He, an expert in these confrontations, is easily able to judge from her responses whether or not she's dubious; the danger is in her going along with the proposal but, to be sure, checking with the police, who would contact their Special Branch, who would go to MI5. If there's doubt, the agent uses stage-dressing. He takes the mark to meet a "high government official." This could be in an impressive office with a phony policeman on the door. Or he takes her to the House of Commons, where their man is just leaving, so that they talk in a taxi. Or a look-alike for a well-known Member of Parliament is used, the meeting place helpfully dim. Whichever, the mark is impressed with the high level of it all, as well as the intrigue and glamour. She accepts without question the need for total secrecy, agrees to abide by agent's orders and decisions.

The whole scheme was entirely possible, Apple agreed. The KGB only needed to set up the first chapter of Blushers Anonymous. The rest would be started by innocents, and all the KGB had to do was put an agent in each. Simple.

Possible indeed, Apple mused, especially with that tailing bit last night. If it had been real. So what now? Should he wait for another pointer/sign/clue before telling Angus Watkin of his suspicion, or should he tell him anyway?

Glancing aside at his Control's dull profile, Apple decided a fast negative. In the instant, his notion of BA being a Red plot had gone back to an absurdity. He could imagine Watkin, having heard him out, asking an icy and demolishing, "I beg your pardon? *What* Anonymous?"

Apple slumped into glumness. He beat back with regret the hovering reveries of himself being congratulated and promoted for having smashed this vast international conspiracy; of being patronising with Angus Watkin; and, espionage personnel having to hide their light from the public gaze, of going clandestinely to Buckingham Palace to receive a medal or two from the Queen, with whom he has a cozy chat.

Like a hobbled goat, the conference limped on. No one was in a hurry. It was as though the spy business was having a slack season. Between points on the agenda the German told a dirty joke or the Norwegian chanted a limerick. Once, the Turk had to be nudged out of a doze.

Apple unslumped. He brought himself back to medium cheer by picking up with glee, as if it were a stumbled enemy, every grammatical error his Control made while using a foreign language. When, however, on these occasions, the other interpreters glanced across at him in the camaraderie of superior knowledge, he glazed his eyes blank.

At five o'clock the meeting broke up for the day. Apple and Angus Watkin left Bigelow Titles together, this being commanded by Watkin by a faint jerk of his head. He asked as they walked to the stairs, "Are you all right, Porter?"

"Perfectly, sir."

"For a while back there you were twitching like the victim of some tedious disease."

"Indigestion, sir," Apple said smoothly. "I bolted a junkfood lunch."

With a hint of approval nearly gleaming through the matt grey facade, Angus Watkin said, "Excellent, Porter. I like to see you showing a modicum of deceit. You must do it more often."

They started down the stairs. "Deceit, sir?"

"Your lie about bolting junkfood. Told, of course, to state how much you suffer in your determination to be prompt, efficient. You are never late, Porter, and that spot on your tie is undoubtedly soy sauce."

"Yes, I was lying, sir," Apple said, telling himself he ought to have known better. "I'm trying to get in a bit of practice whenever I can."

"That's another lie," Watkin said. "Excellent again."

Mumbling, Apple looked down at his boring tie. Angus Watkin said, "No, Porter, there's no spot. But you did bear the spoor of a Chinese restaurant. In an enclosed space it's good for about two hours, as opposed to four for an Indian, three for a Greek, and some fourteen minutes for a British."

They came into the lobby and stopped. With others from the conference going past, Watkin asked, "And the real reason for those disease symptoms?"

Apple, going overboard into truth: "I must've been daydreaming, sir."

"There was nothing being said by our colleagues that struck you as peculiar?"

"No, sir."

"Perhaps, Porter, there's something on your mind."

Apple's hesitation was so scant, the measure of half a gasp, that he was almost unaware of it himself—until, while shaking his head, he saw that it had been noted by Angus Watkin, who did a Kodak blink.

Apple offered what was true most of the time. "I was wondering, sir, when you were going to send me out again on active service."

"Were you really?" his Control said as if agreeing to listen to a funny anecdote. "Myself, I rarely waste time on idle conjecture, since I lack the ability to read the minds of others. Perhaps you don't have that lack, Porter."

"I do, sir."

"You will be sent out when fate or fortune presents us with an endeavour in which your particular talents can be put to work." He used the glib tone of mothers answering their toddlers' why why whys. "Good day, Porter."

"Er—good day, sir," Apple said, backing off from his immobile, expressionless chief. "Good day."

Angus Watkin looked the other way. Apple, crushed, left. He strode tautly along the street, hating with true devotion, muttering to himself about what he was going to do to the odious Watkin one of these fine days if someone didn't shoot the bastard first or if he didn't expire from excess of emotion.

Apple was still muttering when, turning a corner, he came within sight of Ethel and saw a man sitting on her running-board.

Like a lawyer who gets hired by the other side in mid-trial, Apple had an instant and easy change of goal for his ire. The latest mental arrow he had been about to shoot at Angus Watkin he sent flying toward the trespasser. His feelings then underwent another rapid switch as, getting closer, he saw that the man was white-haired Jasper, member of Blushers Anonymous.

The shriek sensation caused by a cold key dropped down the back, which trick has given much pleasure to the droppers without ever managing to stop a nose-bleed, came to Apple as he walked on. He scratched his spine. Inside, he felt out of balance. His mind was nodding at coincidence while asking if this was that awaited sign/clue/pointer.

Jasper saw him, got up. He settled his square spectacles, stepped forward with stretching smile and extended hand, said, "There you are, old man. Thought you'd never show up."

Apple's greeting and handshake were both flabby, lacking form. The smile he made no attempt to return. He asked a flat, gauche "What's wrong?"

Unheedful, Jasper talked on, his manner suggesting that not only had they known each other for countless years, but had gone through hellfire together.

". . . so I said to myself if that's not old Appleton's car I'm a Dutch barge. I didn't know the licence number, naturally, but I knew there couldn't be two old taxis painted as crazily as this one. Anyway, with time to fill in, waiting for the little woman, I . . ."

No, Apple thought, settling to normal except for a dirge of disappointment, this character could hardly be part of a Communist conspiracy. He and the approach were too blatant. Or could that (dirge holding) be the allayer?

". . . when I mentioned FVMT to you last night. But I

don't know if I went into details. I couldn't, could I, as
we're not supposed to talk about our private lives."

"Mmm," Apple non-committed. He didn't recall any
talk of a FVMT, which sent his dirge into a cautious
retreat.

"The secrecy has no sense to it," Jasper said. "Don't
you agree, Appleton?"

"Oh, I don't know."

"I, frankly, am quite willing to tell you all you want to
know about me."

Apple said, "Best not to, though. I think we should
stick to the rules, at least for the time being."

Jasper looked to have a dirge of his own. He said,
"Oh."

"Why don't you tell me all about FVMT instead. Is it
another Blushers Anonymous kind of thing?"

Brightening like someone who sees the rooftops of
home, Jasper said, "No, the letters stand for Friends of
Venerable Motorised Vehicles. Not bad, eh?"

Apple nodded happily. "Neat, Jasper."

"Thank you."

"Is it a big group?"

"So far, no. It's just me."

Apple, smiling: "Ah yes."

"I thought of it last night while talking to you."

"Well now, Jasper, that's most interesting."

"The thing is, there're lots of people who love old
crocks but don't own one themselves, such as myself. So
why shouldn't they have an appreciation society?"

"No reason whatever. I'm all for it."

"Fine," Jasper said. "Seeing your car here today by
accident has made me all the keener. I'm going to think
out the mechanics of the thing. So look, if you give me
your address and telephone number, I'll be in touch with
you the minute I've got the show on the road."

Apple pointed out that since they would be meeting at Meen Hall tomorrow night, and regularly thereafter, information could be passed on then. "Right?"

His back to home's rooftops, Jasper said, "Oh. Right. Quite."

"Good luck with those mechanics."

Cheering: "Thank you."

Apple drove off dirgeless. He was, however, unconvinced. His emotions were restrainedly rubbing their hands together, his logic was shaking its head with glad emphasis.

Apple decided not to think about it anymore. Jasper was almost certainly a harmless oddball along the lines of Lady Barre (another innocent, surely) who was merely being sociable.

So, decision made and nodded into place, Apple, heading for Bloomsbury, thought: He follows me doggedly out of last night's meeting, he waits around today for hours and hours, he invents FVMT as a way of maintaining contact, he offers to tell about himself in order to get the same in return, he tries craftily to get address and telephone number.

Apple also thought: He insults Ethel last night because he couldn't care less about building up a relationship with her owner, he kills time today by sitting on her to rest or to earn looks of envy from passers-by, he comes up with the pleasant idea of FVMT, he is prepared to be open and honest about himself, he routinely asks for an address.

The metaphorical hand-rubbing and head-shaking went on until, after leaving Ethel in the underground parking garage, Apple walked to nearby Harlequin Mansions. The apartment building was as elegant as a healthy and pampered octogenarian ought to be.

Apple's flat had large rooms with high ceilings, as

though the architect had had a future tenant in mind. The tenant prowled, looking into cupboards and nooks while telling himself he was most assuredly not thinking about Blushers Anonymous being a Red plot.

And while not thinking thus, Apple noted the reminder that the non-plotters didn't necessarily have to be from behind a certain heavy metal-type curtain. They could be friends in quotes. When things were slow in the spook racket, Controls sometimes kept their people occupied and in practice by setting up all manner of curious endeavours, malignant or benign.

Eventually, it occurred to Apple to ask, What am I doing? This was when for the second time he caught himself peering into the drawer of the hall hatstand. The answer came as, I'm looking for something, obviously.

Apple closed the drawer, cogitated, remembered. He was looking for Ethel's papers.

Ashamed, charging himself with being less concerned about Ethel than with the wild, outside possibility of some kind of spy scheme, Apple let himself out of the flat. He went back in and straight to his writing-desk in the living room. His face was alive with interest. He searched, meanwhile picturing the map-fold document, called a log-book, which formed the deeds of UK vehicles. Any moment now he expected it to appear.

It stayed absent.

Humming to balance the fact that his features had lost their animation, like arriving patrons being told the bar was closed, Apple went into his bedroom. From the wardrobe he took a suitcase. It had a false top. He shook out of it his private papers and began to sift.

There was a photograph of himself, stark naked, lying on a bearskin rug, aged six months. There were the eighteen poems he had written to eighteen women, declaring his undying love, forsaking all others, in seventeen of

them. There were family letters of moment. There was
the first money he ever earned, a ten-shilling note for
taking back a cat he had found in its garden. There was
the stub of the money-order for ten shillings which he
had sent anonymously to the cat-owner.

In a separate envelope were souvenirs of the times
Apple had been out in the field as an espionage operative. He had the ticket he bought on a bus when he was
following a mark, who on alighting was then tailed by
another agent, ending Apple's involvement. He had the
quarantine certificate for his dog Monico (lodged in the
country), whom he had brought back from what he
thought of as That Amusing Little Business in Ibiza.
There was the cigarette he had accepted from a beautiful female agent during an exchange of signals when he
was supposed to have said, "No, thanks, I don't smoke."

But there was no log-book.

Suitcase put away, Apple searched in all the possible
places. Realising that he had ended his hum, he started it
again, pitch higher than before, a muffled wail that made
his lips tingle. Once more he went through the desk,
roughly.

It was as Apple was stepping down from a chair after
having looked in the ceiling light that he thought of the
cottage. That, he told himself, was where the log-book
must be. Had to be. Was forced to be because there was
nowhere else it could be.

Falsifying a laugh of relief, Apple began to pace.

TWO

The brown paper bag had roughly cut holes for eyes and a tattered slit as a mouth. The man who was wearing the bag on his head stood on the platform, at attention, as relaxed as a bent rapier, as responsive as bacon. Questions from the floor he fielded with monosyllables and grunts.

There being a dozen new members this evening, Lady Barre had moved the action to Meen Hall's proper end. Perky with success, it seemed, she stood well aside, sharing her attention between the garrulous Sam and the forty-odd people who filled scatteredly the seating's near half.

Apple sat toward the back. This was mainly to avoid Jasper, whose signal to join him on the front row Apple had pretended not to see; partly because he had a slight headache from a poor night's sleep and a dreary afternoon's stint of playing interpreter at the spymaster conference. Nor was he made to feel any better by the fact that Wendy had failed to show up this evening.

"And tell me, Sam," someone asked, "do you get a buzzing in your ears at the same time?"

Sam shook his bag. "No."

Someone else: "Can things you read in books and newspapers and so on make you blush?"

Sam shuddered. "Yes."

Apple let his attention wander in order to stop feeling

superior to the sorely afflicted Sam. He had a second scan over the newcomers, five of whom were women.

All were aged from forty upwards, all by their clothing and manner were of the professional or leisure class, all had the same nervous hands as the two men, same type, who had made it into the hall and then, fiery red, had fled for the outdoors as though they were going to be asked to sing.

What intrigued Apple was that a good number of the newcomers were already in some degree of paper-baggery. Two of the women wore hats with thickish veils, one had her hair brushed forward to semi-hide her face. Two of the men had beards which had a decided appearance of falseness, another pair wore dark glasses, one had on a floppy cap that was pulled down almost to the bridge of his nose.

While Apple was wondering if they were genuine sufferers or had merely attended out of curiosity, or whatever, he heard a rearward sound. Lady Barre looked back, smiled, went to the hall's rear as Apple turned. He also smiled.

Wendy had come in from the passage. She wore the same black raincoat and looked just as fetching. After she and Lady Barre had shaken hands they settled to a whispering. Apple only caught Wendy's apology for being late.

"Good evening, Appleton."

He turned back front as Jennifer Rolph sank into the seat at his side. In the same quiet tone she herself had used, which had a nice spy-like hush to it, he returned the greeting and said, "Your hair looks nice, Jen." It was a statement of fact.

Blinking like a culprit Jennifer said, "Well, thank you. What a shame I can't give a maidenly blush."

"You mean because you're not a—um—?"

"A blusher, no. I'm not all that maidenly, either, truth to tell. And it was sweet of you to hold back from suggesting it yourself."

As Apple was opening his mouth to answer with he didn't know what, at the same time fearing/expecting an attack of heat and getting ready to climb into a sunrocket, Jennifer took hold of his wrist.

She squeezed hard. In a low, urgent voice she told him about the Ekans reptile of the Lower Congo that could kill you by wrapping itself backwards around a pressure point.

His interest aroused at this piece of information, Apple was about to offer in return that dogs always circled before lying down because ancestors had done so to make a nest, when Jennifer asked, releasing his wrist:

"That stopped an attack, didn't it?"

Apple sat back. He tested, nodded. "It did, by God."

"One of our new people gave me the trick. It has little repeat effect, unfortunately, but we do seem to be getting somewhere with BA, I think."

"I think so as well, Jen."

She tapped her notebook. "Anyway, I just came to tell you that you're on soon, after the next one."

"Good," Apple said honestly.

"Try not to get tense."

"It's okay. I've had audiences before, when giving lectures."

There was a patter of embarrassed applause as Bag Sam left the platform. With an excuse-me Jennifer got up. She called out, "Now it's Marilyn."

A girl in her teens or just out, Marilyn lasted one minute. That was how long it took her, apparently, to realise that she couldn't go through with the ordeal of being looked at by so many people at the same time. She went onto the platform, stared around as wide of eye as though every face were hideous, scurried back to her seat.

Everyone began to talk about the weather. Above the rumble Jennifer called, "Appleton, please."

As Apple walked forward he noted that Wendy was joining the audience, taking a seat beside Newspaper Norman, and, as he turned in front of the platform on which he had no intentions of standing, that Lady Barre had stayed at the exit, whence she watched in the stance of a fond mother at the school play.

Quiet crept in. Prepared, hands pocketed with the thumbs out in true lecturer fashion, Apple said, "All right, ladies and gentlemen. Questions, please."

A man, one eye narrowed suspiciously, asked, "Are you sure you're a blusher?"

"Petit-mal, yes. Speaking like this doesn't bother me greatly because of one of those gimmicks that we all have. And I shall now pass it on to you."

He explained that what you had to do in these circumstances was pretend the situation was reversed. You were audience, audience was centre of attention. So you chose a face and spoke to it until its owner looked away, as inevitably he did, whereupon you moved on to another face.

"It won't work for you immediately, but it will with time and practice."

From the audience came murmurs of appreciation and a speckle of handclaps. Apple looked at Wendy with a smile, which she returned while making a gesture of thanks.

The questioning began. Apple was honest with his answers. Yes, he blushed when alone. No, he was not married nor had he ever been close to entering that state. Yes, his uncommon height had not made his affliction any easier. Yes, he thought diet may have some bearing on the condition.

Jasper raised his hand. He asked, "What type of work do you do, Appleton?"

Because in Training Six he had learned the body-language poses that suggested honesty, Apple unpocketed his hands and clasped them on his breastbone. He said, "I'm a scientist."

He looked at a woman. She looked away immediately. He next chose a man, who took five seconds to lower his eyes. He looked at Jasper, who asked, "What kind of scientist?"

From the back Lady Barre called, "You mustn't answer if it's giving too much away."

"No problem," Apple said easily. "Let's put it that I work in a laboratory." He dropped his hands. "Next question, please."

When, his session over, Apple left the front he went to where Wendy was sitting. There being no space beside her, he took the chair to her rear. She swivelled around and they began a whispered discussion of his public-speaking gimmick. That ended when they were hissed at for silence.

Over the following half hour, between sympathising with those up front and having brief exchanges with Wendy, Apple wondered what would result from his lie, which he hadn't known he was going to make. He had thought he had given up on the BA-as-plot foolishness.

Apple felt fine, sharp, vital; felt the devilish and unpredictable character he had always suspected he could be if he would only give himself the chance.

Jennifer called out another name. Apple leaned toward Wendy. "Listen," he said close to her ear, whose shape he liked. "It's getting near the end. How about if we slide away now and have a drink somewhere?" The suggestion was partly to make himself not too available, suspiciously available, to anyone who might be an enemy.

Wendy said, "Oh, I don't know."

"I have another gimmick I'd like to tell you about."

"Well, okay then. One drink. I'm having an early night."

While the new speaker was going forward, Apple and Wendy got up into the illicit-leaver's crouch. They went to the passage, where Lady Barre said she hoped they weren't giving up. "Faint heart never won fair skin, y'know." She laughed. "Get it?"

They said they did and Wendy enthused about Blushers Anonymous. Lady Barre patted her arm while telling Apple, "You have a truly delightful car."

"I didn't know you'd seen her."

"Well, I haven't, actually. Jasper was telling me about it. You must promise to give me a ride."

"With pleasure. Whenever you like."

"We'll be in touch, Appleton," Lady Barre said, slapping a hank of hair away from her face. "Good night to you both."

They said good night and Wendy added, "Congratulations on the way BA keeps growing."

"Isn't it wonderful? In fact it's quite remarkable."

"Yes," Apple said. "It is."

The pub, crowded, was as placid as a kindergarten bunfight. Men who could have been dockers or gangsters, women who could have been harlots or social workers or just plain mums, they stood three deep at the bar wearing flushes that were straight, not morbid, paid for glass by glass.

In a corner, Apple and Wendy went on with their semi-yelled conversation about jobs, he sipping sherry on the rocks, she with a gin and tonic. Apple kept an unobtrusive eye on the door. He was hoping they had been followed and still wondering if there was significance in the person, rendered formless by distance, who had appeared outside Meen Hall on his last look back.

The reason Apple had skirted around to the subject of jobs was so he could now say, "Several BA members have asked me about my work. I like the friendly interest."

"Everyone wants to know what the other man does."

"Though in this case maybe they think it might have a bearing on my blushing."

Wendy said, "Well, it could, of course."

"You've had the same sort of thing, BA members asking you about your job?"

"Why, yes, as it happens."

To lessen the distance their words had to travel, Apple increased his stoop, the one he always adopted when standing with someone shorter than himself, which meant ninety-nine times out of a hundred. Only three or four inches now separated their faces. The intimacy felt so soothing and affectionate that it made him smile. Wendy smiled back.

"This is fun," she said.

"Seconded and passed."

The door could be heard opening. Apple decided it would be a shame to destroy this warming togetherness, therefore didn't look around, which caused him to sigh because of his lack of professionalism. Wendy sighed back.

She said, "Frankly, I get bored with shop talk."

Apple asked, "Is that what you told Lady Barre when she asked you about your work?"

"Don't remember. In fact, I don't remember who was asking me. Could've been Lady B."

Not pressing, since that would seem peculiar, Apple

changed the subject again and concentrated on the business of trying to cultivate an interesting and pretty girl.
He managed to resist the urge to stroke her urchin-cut
hair.

They finished their drinks. Wendy declined to have
another for the road. She also declined, when they were
leaving, to go somewhere off the beaten track for supper:
"I really do want an early night."

Apple, scanning around the crowd as he followed her
out and seeing no one even vaguely familiar, asked,
"How about if we get together tomorrow evening?"

"I'm busy from eightish. Before that would be okay,
though. I leave work at four. We could meet for a coffee."

They set off along the street and Apple, after a glance
behind, snapped his fingers. "Tea," he said. "How'd you
like to come to tea in my country cottage?"

"That sounds good."

"I can have you back long before eight."

They settled details as they walked, Apple throwing
more casual glances behind and still gaining nothing.
Wendy asked if there was something wrong with his
neck. He said Meen Hall was draughty, which got them
back to the topic of Blushers Anonymous and its founder.

Wendy said, "Don't you think Lady B's eccentric manner and clothing are a bit overdone?"

"Heavy, yes. But likeable."

"It's as if she was perfectly aware of the effect, like an
actress."

Apple said, "Maybe she was one. The old story of
chorus girl and titled stage-door Johnny."

"No, she's the aristocrat. Sir Jack was a miner's son
who got knighted for giving a fortune to charity. He
invented all kinds of gadgets, I understand."

They stopped in front of a tall house, one of an unbro-
ken row. The door, up steps, stood open, showing a drab

interior. Wendy said this was where she had her bed-sitter.

"Very respectable, sad to relate, like the district. All the dangerous-looking people around here turn out to be shopclerks or choirmasters or off-duty policewomen."

Emboldened by his success with the tea date, Apple said, "And I look respectable, but . . ."

Laughing, Wendy started up the steps. "Till tomorrow."

Apple turned away. Wendy he stopped thinking about only when he came to within sight of Meen Hall, on the opposite side of the street. Then, without much idea of what he was doing, but not considering it objectively in case he felt stupid, he stood in shadow beside a large-bodied van that looked as though it had put down roots.

Blushers Anonymous meeting over, people were gathered in aftertalk outside the building. Among the unknowns were Newspaper Norman, Jasper, Jennifer Rolph and Lady Barre. Soon those two women, accompanied by one of the new members, a tall man with silvery hair, broke off from the mass and came this way. They got into an unkempt-looking Bentley, Jennifer at the wheel, others behind. They moved off, went past.

Probably just giving the guy a lift home, Apple thought tediously. He stood on, watching.

Next to leave was Jasper. He also came in this direction, striding with swinging arms like a sergeant-major showing new recruits what he has in mind. After fifty yards he began to come across the street.

Neatly Apple glided backwards beside the van's body. He continued moving in reverse so that by the time Jasper appeared to him again, stepping over the kerb from between two parked cars, he was at the front of the vehicle. He sidled into the gutter.

As Apple knew from Training Four in relation to situations such as this, to assume that your mark is going to do the apparent is naive. He might recross the street suddenly, he might circle your vehicle from the rear. So Apple waited until the approaching footfalls were loud, then, as also learned in Four, bent his body over severely in order to take his head within inches of the tarmac. Underneath the van Apple could see Jasper's feet and ankles. He watched them come closer. Since they stayed in the same path, he began to move around the van, in the roadway, though maintaining his doubled-up pose so as to keep nether Jasper in view. It wasn't easy. Even with a balancing hand on the ground, it wasn't easy.

Jasper reached the front and went on. Apple straightened. The moment he was fully upright he saw that he had observers. Across the road, a young couple were watching from the back seat of a car. Fixedly they watched, like hunters, leaning forward, eyes drastic.

Inspired, Apple performed an act of explanation. He bent low again, from the side of his mouth gave out a realistic miaowing sound, rose with a shrug of resignation at how obstinate some cats could be—and went around to the van's other side.

Jasper was in sight farther on. Cheered by his presence of mind back there, Apple set out in pursuit.

Not many operatives, he wouldn't have minded betting, could have come up with that cat bit. His reminder of the absence of operation, let alone that the ploy had served no useful purpose, he ignored as firmly as he was the possibility that his doubled-up progress had looked farcical.

Still marching like a Sousa addict, Jasper turned off Meen Lane. He went along another street, came out onto a commercial road, strode on beside closed shops whose windows were brightly lit. This glow, in addition to the stark lighting above, made Apple take extra precautions.

First he went into the roadway, where traffic passed at a steady drone like grumblers heading for Complaints. Next he bent his knees while walking there. Last he kept his face turned away so that if Jasper glanced back he would see only a profile.

All this was gratifying for Apple, slaking his hunger for spy doings. It pleased him despite the dust and exhaust fumes being blown in his face, despite the ache in his knees and despite the fact that from having his face turned aside he eventually lost sight of the man he was following.

This realised, Apple stopped. He looked around. He noted that he had just passed a milk bar. Reversing, through the steamy window he could see his mark taking a stool at the counter, which he had to himself.

Humming a light refrain at how quickly, easily and professionally he had put matters to rights, Apple retraced his steps further and went through to the pavement. Eight or ten businesses back along from the milk bar he came to an alley. He entered its mouth and stood there in a lean against the wall by the corner, from where he needed merely to bow with a look left to check on where Jasper had settled.

Although wheeled traffic was constant, the foot variety had less to offer. Even so, enough people went by and glanced aside furtively at the man in the alley to maintain his cheer and stop him from growing bored.

Apple speculated on what these people would think he was up to, which made it agreeably difficult for him to speculate on that himself.

A narcotics dealer waiting for a client, Apple was thinking when he heard the faint sound from behind. He might have turned around if he hadn't just been through his business of the cat. In suspense movies they always had that tease routine, a sinister noise that turns out to be a loose shutter when it isn't some harmless feline, and it always made Apple feel stupid for being taken in.

So, instead of looking around, he smiled his superiority. The blow got him on the back of the head. He was unconscious before he hit the ground.

At first Apple thought he had a hangover. There was this pain at the base of his skull, a queasiness in his stomach, a taste in his mouth like a doormat. He realised furthermore, continuing to float below the level of full awareness, that he was lying in the open, concrete below, stars above.

I am sprawled out in a gutter, Apple thought with hope on the hover. I was knocking 'em back like a lord and got as drunk as a count. I had a blonde on each arm but I got fed up with 'em and then passed out. I have been outrageous.

Consciousness returning at a snap, Apple remembered he had been a fool. But he was encouraged more than depressed. The attack, surely, was the strongest sign of all.

He sat up, paused for assessment, got to his feet. The yuck taste in his mouth and his queasiness came, he knew, from having drunk sherry on an empty stomach. The blow on his head came, he was almost certain, from someone who knew what he was doing; knew how to put a man to sleep with the minimum of damage: the pain was bearable; there was no blood coming from the half-egg swelling; his watch told him he had been out for about three minutes, which was short, and the shorter the healthier.

Now Apple realised that his pockets were dangling inside out like ears. He checked everywhere. His wallet and loose money had been taken. In a search of the immediate area, however, he found his wallet, intact contentswise except for cash.

So had he merely been rolled?—Apple wondered. He doubted it because a mugger who was determined enough to knock a man out wouldn't be lax enough to ignore his watch. But there again, the mugger might have been scared off by passers-by.

Apple's next realisation was that the attacker had, in a sense, left part of his calling-card; its size if not its name, but the last might be deduced from the first.

At a smooth pace, not wishing to jolt his head, Apple left the alley and went along the street. Conveniently, there was a public telephone booth on the next corner. Apple went in. While he was feeding the coinslot he didn't have to tell his foot to hold the door an inch ajar to pamper his claustrophobia; it knew.

As always, Apple enjoyed calling in. It wasn't often he got the opportunity to contact Upstairs. When a male voice answered he tried to match its casual calm, quoting his service number and saying, "I'd like an expert, please."

"Department?"

"Wounds."

"How messy is it?"

With a tinge of regret Apple had to admit, "No blood. Just a bash on the head."

"Treatment required?"

"Opinion only. At my pad if possible. Address on file. In twenty mins." He smiled out of affection for his briskness and that cool, pro shortening of the last word.

The man asked, "In twenty what?"

Quietly, Apple said, "Minutes."

"Make it thirty. Good-bye."

His mind seizing on Jasper as he stooped out of the

booth, Apple decided to collect Ethel before checking at the milk bar. He went on. His pace he quickened on finding out that the pain in his head was staying at the same low grind.

Ethel stood waiting near Meen Hall. Apple got in. With his eyes wide in case there was an explosion when he turned the key, he started her up. He drove on with a sigh.

The milk bar was deserted apart from a woman behind the counter drinking from a bottle of beer. Making no comment to himself in respect of Jasper, Apple headed for Bloomsbury.

Ethel garaged, apartment reached, Apple paced around from room to room like a convict back home. He looked in every mirror available and made no attempt to correct his dishevelled appearance or dust the dirt off his clothes. When the flat bell rang he unawarely adopted a harrowed expression.

The man he opened the door to was middle-aged, bulky in a worn overcoat, affable as a vet who had just waded through snow to the wrong farm. "Haunch of venison," he accused.

"I beg your pardon?"

"That's what I was in the middle of."

"Sorry about that."

"Which will do me a fat lot of good."

"This way," Apple said. He led into the living room, where he sat on a low stool. "There you go."

The man stood behind him with a judicial, "Hmmm."

He would, Apple knew, say presently something along the lines of, "The attacker was five feet eleven inches tall, weighed in the region of one hundred and sixty-three pounds, has twenty-twenty vision and as a weapon used a smooth rock in the toe of a stocking."

"Hmmm," the man said again, moving away.

Apple got up. "The verdict?"

"Professional job. Couldn't have done better myself. The blunt instrument was probably a standard cosh."

"And the attacker?"

"Sorry," the man said, not looking sorry. "All reckonings are out of kilter with the likes of you. Too bloody tall."

Apple spent the following morning in bed. That had not been his intention, but within minutes of getting up he found it true what the expert from Wounds had said on leaving: "You'll get a delayed action from that little tap."

After poached egg on toast and milky tea (suitable invalid fare), Apple telephoned the United Kingdom Philological Institute. While sardonically fingering his half-egg lump, he said he would be off work with a touch of autumn fever.

As a senior official of UKPI he had no need to make such calls, but he liked the idea that somebody would worry if he didn't show up, and didn't like the idea of that person worrying. Apple wanted things simple.

In bed, room darkened as though for a concussion patient, he mulled over the situation in respect of the dark side of Blushers Anonymous—which mulling, he slyly told himself, was to keep his mind off Ethel's papers.

The signs he had been reading as perhaps showing that a plot was underway could, Apple allowed, be innocent. Even the attack last night could, stretching a point, have been done by a mugger who had been trained in the finer parts of dirty work in one of the armed services' special units. But it was more likely not a thief's work but just made to look that way with the act of robbery.

The real motive was to get more particulars on this tall

blusher who worked in a laboratory, Apple felt, or who might be lying about his job in order to further his investigations into the possibility of Blushers Anonymous having a dark side.

It was nothing more than feeling, Apple admitted. But the feeling was as strong as an instinct. And one thing was sure: BA as Red Plot no longer seemed absurd.

Apple slept.

Awake at noon he got up and again put on his robe, a panic in foot-square tartan, an Ethelesque consolation for the monotony of his everyday clothes. After a shower and a snack he got into those clothes without his usual downcurve mouth. He left the building feeling fit and perky. He didn't even mind that his lump had almost gone.

In company with Ethel he drove into the West End, where he parked her prominently off Oxford Street, the while not thinking about log-books. He went to Bigelow Titles.

The conference sludged along as before. The Turkish spymaster kept himself awake with difficulty and the Norwegian said whenever he was addressed that he had a terrible hangover. Everyone smiled and got up at coffee-break time, a shapely girl coming in with a tray.

Although successful in getting Angus Watkin away from the pack and following him into a corner, Apple was less so on behalf of his wish for this private word. He failed to make himself tell of his Blushers Anonymous suspicions, which didn't surprise him in the slightest. However, he did manage to ask if he could leave early today.

"Is that, Porter, the reason you were rolling your eyes at me so strangely?"

"Didn't realise it, sir."

Angus Watkin looked into his cup. "One would almost suspect there was something on your mind."

Apple stiffened. "Well, as a matter of actual truth," he said. "There is."

"And what is it, pray?"

No, he couldn't tell his plot idea. But he didn't mind too much, for he was glad at least that he had the courage to admit to being a coward.

"A young lady, sir. I said I'd meet her this afternoon for tea, if I could."

Angus Watkin looked up. "For all I know that might be true. In any case, your presence here is hardly of state-trembling consequence. Leave early you may, Porter."

"Thank you, sir."

"Now do try to stop looking distraught. These people might get the idea we're up to something shady."

"And we're not."

"Alas."

Coffee-break ended and the French spymaster stopped talking to the girl so that he could start drinking his coffee. Apple half congratulated himself.

At the approach to four o'clock, getting a nod from Angus Watkin in answer to his subdued throat-clearing, Apple got up and quietly left. Once down on the street he went at a jog. Ethel was alone. It didn't bother him. At the moment there was quite enough on his mind, what with the darkly pretty Wendy and Ethel's documents.

That Wendy, in jeans and thick sweater, was waiting outside her house gave Apple a charge like a cake with candles. They went on burning because of Wendy's enthusiasm over Ethel and died gracefully away, unblown, only when driver and rear-seat passenger had settled in friendly comfort to the journey.

Near that trip's end there was more enthusiasm, when they stopped at Galling's Farm to pick up Monico, from both girl and dog. A thoroughbred Ibizan hound, Monico looked like a whippet with incipient rickets and a sense of guilt. He had never chased a rabbit.

Two minutes later they were at the cottage, whose crumbly aspect made Wendy smile, whose chintzy-cozy interior made her clap her hands into a hold.

"And look at that gorgeous old hearth," she said. "Let's put a fire on. It's chilly enough."

"Right," Apple said in a businesslike manner. "I'll get around to that in a moment. Also to making tea. But there's something I have to see to first."

"Then while you see to it, Appleton, yours truly will be the firemaker."

He didn't argue, partly because he knew she wanted to do what was forbidden by law in smokeless-zone London, partly because he generally made a mess of fire-lighting, if he didn't burn himself, mostly because he was eager now to get on with that search.

First he went into the den, which would have suited a lion of the literary type, books everywhere (spy fiction predominating). He searched through the drawers of a desk, looked under each corner of the rug, started riffling through books with titles that might be significant—he had a notion that when he brought Ethel's log-book here he had hidden it somewhere clever.

That he had brought it here was sure; more cleverness, a spy-like reversal. Monico lived out this way so his papers were kept in town, Ethel lived in Bloomsbury so her papers were put out here.

Without success, Apple turned the pages of *My Shady Past, Wheels, I Was a Taxi-Dancer, Painted Lady* and *Call Me a Cab, Brenda,* among others. He gave up on the den after looking under seat cushions.

When he went into the parlour the fire was burning

like a burst of laughter. From the kitchen Wendy called, "I've found some stale bread. I'm making toast."

"Great," Apple said absently, heading for the staircase. He went up at a run. His spare room ignored (it wouldn't be there), likewise the bathroom, he started on the master bedroom. He looked in every possible hiding place as well as the unlikely. He looked with care. His eyes probed and his mind tried to make a connexion. Sweat came out on his top lip as if to help.

By the time Wendy called up that tea was ready Apple had almost run out of crannies. The remainder he swept through in grimness and then went downstairs. The table was elegantly set for refreshments.

Teapot poised, Wendy asked, "How'm I doing?"

"Terrific."

"You look fed up, Appleton. Did I bring out the wrong china or something?"

Apple shook his head while turning toward the fire. He asked, "Where'd you find the wood?"

"In the log-box, of course."

"Of course." He went around beside the fireplace to the tall wooden bin. When, with difficulty, he had eased it sideways off the floor, he found an envelope underneath, and when with clumsy fingers he had opened it, he found the log-book. He went creaky at the knees with relief.

"Yes, really terrific, Wendy," he said, joining her at the table. He flapped the document. "I couldn't remember where I'd put this."

"Must be the winning ticket on a big lottery."

Apple began to explain, after he had bitten into a slice of toast coated with lemon marmalade the way another man might knock back a fast brandy. He finished, "They're a load of car snobs at ALTOG but I'm determined to join."

"It would be so good for Ethel."

"Perhaps you're right."

Wendy pointed. "Careful."

Looking down Apple saw that in his unsteadiness he had spilled tea from his cup. Some of the mild spillage was on the log-book. Unconcernedly he started mopping up with a paper napkin. The napkin turned black at the same time as the lettering on the document smudged.

Apple stared in horror. He didn't need his Training Seven knowledge to realise that the log-book was a forgery.

Only vaguely was Apple aware of the rest of the meal, of closing up the cottage, returning Monico to Farmer Galling and driving back to town.

So as not to be a downer, he told Wendy that the document was a copy (made in the days before photocopy machines existed) so there was not a thing to worry about. He acted brightness. Inside he fretted, Was Ethel illegitimate? Was she, in fact, the original and genuine Ethel? Would it prove impossible to get real papers?

He dropped Wendy off outside her house. Although they exchanged telephone numbers and Wendy eulogized the outing, Apple was aware that, despite his bright facade, their date had not finished up an outrageous success. Nor at the moment was he in the mood to suggest another. He had a case of the hurry-ups.

Within minutes of driving away from Wendy's he was stopping by a street telephone booth. It was occupied. He dithered, decided to wait patiently, alighted and stood with arms folded where he could be seen by the caller, an older man in a jogging suit that dangled on a skinny frame.

Apple moved closer, glaring his patience. When the man got no return to his weak smile and found that he could get no further away because of the glass wall at his back, he ended his call and came out jogging.

Pleased with the way he had kept placid, Apple rumpled inside. He got through to Upstairs. Preliminaries over, he said, "I want an expert, please." He spoke with extra briskness as what he was trying on—using Upstairs for personal reasons—was against the regulations.

"Wounds?" the voice asked. It was the same duty officer as the last time.

"Documents," Apple said. "He can come to my place, or, if it's more convenient, I can meet him somewhere."

"Usually there's not much hurry with Documents."

"There is today."

The line went dead after "Call back in ten minutes."

It seemed like a hundred and ten. But at least during the wait Apple resolved one of his disturbing questions: whether or not his pseudo ex-taxi was the genuine Ethel.

In the sixties a group of Western espionage operatives, off duty and bored, had made a bet as to who could locate the notorious Ethel first. The winner, a Canadian, time two hours, scratched his initials on the radiator. They, sometime in the following days, were joined by the letters USSR, presumably put there by the KGB to say, in essence, We know everything that's going on. Apple had always secretly believed that Angus Watkin had arranged the addition for reasons best known only to his own twisted mind.

Both sets of initials were there, Apple discovered. He had known they would be but he ignored that as devoutly as he was ignoring that he had invented the worrisome question in the first place, to give himself something to be relieved about.

He went back in the booth and called Upstairs. The duty officer said, "Available now. Ready to absorb?" He gave information, including rendezvous, physical description and identification signals.

"Thank you," Apple brisked. "Over and out."

"So long."

Rendezvous was a pub in Camden Town. Apple drove there swiftly, scraped tyres on the kerb in parking, needed to dart back because he had forgotten to lock up.

After a pause outside to slow himself down, he strolled in. Early evening, there were few people in the gaunt room, which stated its social position as surely as would a person, by dress, here that being curtains and a carpet.

The woman who matched the description ("Sixty, dumpy, nice clothes, hat with red rose") sat alone at a table. Her manner and her style played suburban matron waits for nephew.

Apple went across. At the table he said, "I hope I'm not too late this week."

The woman whom he had been told to call Doc looked up with an imp grin. "And what if I said I didn't know what you were talking about?"

Although pricked with disappointment, Apple smiled back. "So much for signals."

"Sit down, lad. Drink?"

"No, thanks, Doc. I just want you to look at this."

The woman started talking almost before the log-book had been put down in front of her. She recognised the type-face, she said. "Discontinued long ago. Twenty-five years at least. The press belonged to a department of the Special Branch. You know how that lot got started, of course."

The Special Branch was a counter-espionage section within the regular police, whom Angus Watkin called the amateurs, Apple knew. He said so.

Doc nodded. "It was originally called the Special *Irish*

Branch, set up in 1884 to fight the Fenians, forerunners of the Irish Republican Army."

Despite the circumstances, Apple was grateful for the snippet of data and, Doc being obviously a fellow infomaniac, he forgave her for that spoiling of signals.

Tapping the log-book he said, "If it dates back to the time of first registration, this vehicle can't have been officially registered."

"Stolen from factory or dealer."

"So there won't be an original that I can get an official copy of."

"Absolutely not," Doc said. "Is it important?"

As personal use of Upstairs' many-faceted amenities was unkosher, and as he couldn't resist showing off, and as Doc seemed to be eager for shoptalk, Apple, employing a casualness that hinted at understatement, said, "Fairly so. You've been a great help. This little caper I'm on will now advance."

Doc shuffled herself happily like a gossip's audience. "Are you sure you wouldn't like a drink?"

Apple had a sherry on the rocks. He wasn't in the mood and he found it hard to talk when he was in the process of accepting that Ethel was indeed illegitimate and could never become a member of the Antique London Taxicab Owners Guild; but Doc, he realised, was a faceless one, a specialist who, like himself, got assignments rarely and so must have been pleased to have been sent to this meeting, such as it was. Therefore Apple, lingering, played operative in the field.

Leaving at last, treacherous log-book thrust into his pocket any old how, Apple drove in pale gloom to Bloomsbury. He left Ethel with an extra pat.

His telephone was ringing as he approached the flat door. Knowing it would only stop at the last moment if he hurried, he entered slowly, walked slowly to the living room and to the corner table, slowly reached down to the telephone. The ringing stopped.

Gratified at having his gloom fed, Apple crossed to the writing desk. While thrusting the log-book into a pigeon-hole it occurred to him that there was a solution to Ethel's dilemma. It would not cancel her bastardy (which he would make sure stayed a steel-bound secret), but it would, definitely, hide that fact in the eyes of the world as well as make membership of ALTOG a possibility.

The telephone rang.

Apple went over and answered. The caller was Lady Barre. She said, "You're a hard man to get hold of, Appleton. This isn't the first time I've rung you."

"I come and go," Apple said, putting a social-butterfly weariness into his voice to disguise how interesting/stimulating he found this call.

"Please forgive the last-minuteness, but I'm tossing a little soirée this evening at short notice and I wondered if you'd care to come."

"I'd love to."

"Wonderful," Lady Barre said. "I'm staying at Viceroy House, if you know it."

He did, Apple said. He disconnected after collecting a time, plus a suite number in the apartment-hotel which had been one of the town bases of Britain's moneyed classes since India reluctantly became a prong in the crown. He even remembered to say thank you.

Humming like a burglar on his way out, Apple strolled to the window. He looked down at the street, where lights sprinkled the dusk, where people and cars moved with purpose.

Apple told himself that if he could pull off a coup in respect of a certain organization, he might have enough clout to get Upstairs to create for him one of its modern technology-wrought masterpieces of forgery.

Viceroy House had a quasi-Greek facade, like the waiters at that little place everyone knows of. The lobby was done in Victorian Drawing Room, with antimacassars and potted palms, whatnots and gewgaws, Salon art and tassles. The ambience dripped discretion lavishly.

As Apple was moving through the scattering of tweedy women with thin daughters and armyfied men with port noses, heading for the reception desk, he saw a false beard. It was on a tall man whose impeccable tailoring caused Apple to immediately dub him Savile Row. He had been one of the newcomers at the last Blushers Anonymous meeting.

Changing course, Apple followed the man to a broad staircase. They went up one behind the other. On the next flight Apple caught up, ascended alongside.

He said, "Good evening. Going to Lady B's?"

The man shied away slightly like a dullard pony. Recovered, he said with a loftiness to match his height, "Ah yes. The scientist. Good evening."

"Appleton's the name."

"Yes, I am going to Lady Barre's."

"I imagine she'll be an old friend of yours."

"No, she won't," Savile Row said. "I do wish they'd put lifts in these old buildings."

Inspired, Apple said, "They manage things better in Russia." It didn't matter that the response was a shrug. The idea was another of the keys Apple needed, along with the phony profession. If he represented himself around as a man with useful information who was sympathetic toward the Soviet Union, there was no telling what he might attract.

"Don't you think so?" he asked as they went along a

broad corridor between boars' heads and crossed lances. "Hasn't Russia got us all beat?"

"I'm afraid I'm terribly right-wing," Savile Row said with an increase in loftiness. "Excuse me." He hurried on to an open door and barged through it like a Hun.

When Apple got there he saw a spacious living room. It held a score of people, all standing, all holding drinks. Savile Row was accepting a glass of champagne from Jennifer Rolph, who bore a tray.

She smiled as Apple went to her. "Nice to see you, Appleton. Grab one of these."

He did. They talked comfortably, Apple meanwhile having a second scan around. There were, he noted, several of the new members present, among others a woman in dark glasses and a heavy-built man with a red wig.

"Must labour on," Jennifer said. "Take this last drink to help me out, mmm?"

His glass emptied and exchanged for a full one, Apple turned. He came chin to hairline with Jasper, who, busily nose-twitching his square spectacles, said, "Got to get together, you and I, old man."

"We are together."

"For a long private talk, I mean."

"When I come back from my holidays in Moscow."

"Portugal. That's the place for me. Nowhere in the world like Lisbon. Ever been there?"

Apple put a hand to the back of his head. "I can't recall a thing since I got a bash the other night."

"Myself, I don't go to many," Jasper said, looking around. "But this bash is nice."

"Very neat," Apple said. He drained his glass. Jasper took it and moved away with "I'll fill us up."

Wearing an angelic smile Apple strolled on, to circulate like a good guest should. He warned himself to take it easy on the champagne, considering that he had already had a sherry this afternoon with Doc.

After circling a couch Apple made up a triangle with two strangers, older women of the artsy-craftsy school, all scarves and bangles. In answer to Apple's question they said they had known Minnie Barre since God had a newspaper round. Apple, determined to be likeable, asked what she had been doing in those days.

One woman said, "Trying to help what the Victorians called fallen women."

Apple shook his head. "Edwardians. Prostitutes were earlier euphemised as *unfortunates.*"

"Oh?" the women unisoned coldly. Turning to each other they began to talk about Christmas.

Apple might have joined in, except for noticing Wendy. Their exchange of mimed greetings over, she signalled that she needed help. She was being talked at by a man whose gesturing hands were mere inches from her breasts, as though he were a juggler in want of something to practice with.

Apple felt knightly. "Excuse me," he said to the two women, who ignored him like a faux pas. Amused at how involved people got in Christmas, he sidled away. More people having come in, the crowd was denser, noisier.

"There you are," Lady Barre said, appearing in his path. She had two glasses, one of which she thrust to him. "We haven't got the party spirit yet, have we?"

"I'm having a fine time," Apple said, which, he realised, was true, and it shouldn't be, he scolded. He was here on business, not pleasure. He grinned. "Yes, really fine."

"Drinky drinky."

He drank. Lady Barre, who wore a black velvet version of overalls and a single string of pearls, said, "You mustn't be embarrassed, young Appleton. Relax. Get loose."

Apple dangled one arm. "I am."

"What we'll have to do very soon, you and I, is have a talk. The way to a cure for you may be for you to tell it all. Get it all out. Tell everything about yourself, no matter how intimate or confidential."

"Good idea. Maybe when I come back from Moscow."

"Oh, don't go there, dear," Lady Barre said. She swiped at a dangling hank of hair as if it were a fly. "Moscow's full of bloody Bolshies."

"But I like Russia."

"So do I. Been there millions of times. But Moscow, dear, is drabber than Liverpool on a wet Sunday at this time of year. Try somewhere else. Drinky drinky."

Apple drained his glass. It was taken from him by a hand, which, when Apple swivelled that way, proved to belong to Jasper. He said, passing over a fresh drink, "Sorry I'm late."

Lady Barre asked him if he had just arrived. He said no, he meant with the champagne. She said she didn't know. She had ordered another case. He said she was very generous. She asked him to put it in the kitchen. He left with a fixed smile.

Apple was feeling dizzy. He semi-listened to Lady Barre talk about spilling beans and getting things off one's chest and letting it all hang out, while sipping like an invalid at his champagne.

Next he knew he was sitting on the couch beside Savile Row, who had been waxing nostalgic, it seemed. He said, "Dear old Dunkirk."

Apple shuffled himself alert. He said, "Bet you were in Army Intelligence."

"Lost your money. I was a boffin."

Which, Apple grasped, was wartime slang for backroomers who worked on codes, inventions, tricks noble and dirty, schemes. He said, "Still at it, I suppose, eh, Sav?"

The man said sadly, "Cosmetics."

Which, Apple saw, could be a lie. He asked, "Anyone shown interest in your work lately?"

"Only you."

"Are you sure? Hasn't someone been asking nosy questions about your racket?"

"I don't understand you, sir," Savile Row said. "Excuse me." He got up, moved away.

After emptying and putting down the glass he had found in his hand, Apple followed. He was not about to waste this gilt opportunity: the man was evasive. He caught up as Savile Row was settling onto a vacant chair between the woman with sunglasses and the man under a wig. They were talking about their gardens.

Apple, who knew nothing of flora, stood in front of the trio listening with poignant, red eyes and a forgiving smile. It was some dreamy time before he was cued to his task by hearing a reference to "wonderful reds."

"Right," he said sharply, staring down at the three. "It's all a matter of equality." He got their attention and, by raising his voice, hoped to get that of those nearby. "Yes, it's all on one level in the dear old USSR."

The sunglasses woman smiled up at him. "That's true. It's nice to hear it recognised."

"Precisely," Apple said in a small shout. "Anyone can recognise that the comrade bit is a load of rubbish."

"What?"

"Soviet society has three distinct divisions. There are about two hundred and fifty million people in the working class. Then you have sixteen million members of the Communist Party. Then you have about three-quarters

of a million top types, the politicos and technocrats and
so on."

Apple paused. He wondered if he was doing this right.
But, since what he was saying was nothing more than the
nude truth, he must be doing fine. He went on in a quiet
yell:

"If you're at the top you can have almost anything—
luxury car, foreign travel, good address, country dacha,
shopping in special stores. In the middle you will have
certain privileges, such as a flat of your own, maybe a car,
more money so you can buy on the black market. If
you're at the bottom, you can't even buy a ticket for the
ballet."

The woman lifted her sunglasses to glare. She accused,
"That's a gross simplification."

"Yes, there are levels within levels, as in all societies,
but those're the three big ones."

"That's not what I meant."

Again Apple wondered if he had got matters confused.
The woman seemed angry with him, and now he noted
that Wiggy and Savvers had drifted away. The conversa-
tional buzz had risen from its hiatus, surpassingly, as
though to make up for lost time. Abruptly, the woman
got up and left.

A spot of fresh air, Apple decided. That's what he
needed. It would clear his head.

Walking as cautiously as a man with a raw egg in his
mouth, Apple went over to a set of French windows. He
opened one side, stepped through. He was on a dark
balcony. Three strides took him to the rail. This was the
rear of Viceroy House, he saw. Above and around him
were lit windows, some thirty feet below were parked
cars.

The air was cool and crisp. After breathing deeply of it
for a moment, gripping the rail, Apple began to feel

worse. His head had more wooziness than before. He started to do deep knee-bends, his arms out in front. The window behind him squeaked mousely. So as not to look stupid he rose quickly from the squat, but didn't turn in time. The shove caught him in the middle of the back. He went head first over the rail.

If the drop had been of undoubted lethal height, Apple, not fighting, would have gone down to his death with a bellow of annoyance. As this drop offered the probability of survival, albeit with a broken bone or two, he fought.

Both hands clawed and scrambled like angry crabs. One took a hard blow on its back, the other met a rail. It met and grabbed. It met and grabbed and held.

But his body was coming down. The reverse position of his arm broke the grip. That, however, took two seconds, during which time Apple was able to establish with his wounded hand a hold on another rail.

All along his vision had been a swirl—lights and the tops of cars. Now, having turned, dangling from one arm, he was looking down onto the balcony below. From what he could see of Lady Barre's, it was deserted and its French window was closed.

Although Apple managed to get a grip with his other hand, he knew he wouldn't be able to climb up, not in his present boozy state, but he agreed that was a plus, that if he wasn't boozy he would be terrified. In any case, he assured himself, even for a sober man it would be a tricky climb.

So what was the answer?—shouts for assistance? No, they were sure to go unheard, and meanwhile his strength was seeping. He had to act at once.

Keeping time with gentle belches, Apple began to swing his body. He sent his legs and trunk under Lady Barre's balcony and out again, under and out. This he kept up until he was reaching for vertical on his last time out. Going back under, he let go, gasping a curse to frighten fate.

He landed with a raucous thud. It hurt his head as much as his feet—though he somehow stayed on them. He was creaking upright with a groan when the French window slapped open, dashing him with light.

Out came an old man in a quilted smoking jacket. As bald as a roared command, his manner and lizard-like features suggested that in his day he had ordered men flogged for having fluff on their uniforms.

Bringing himself to attention, Apple saluted with the official amount of dither. When he had whipped his arm back down he snapped, "All correct, SAH."

The old man held. "What's that?"

"Your orders won the day."

"Oh?"

"Excuse, please," Apple said. He marched around the old man, passed through the French window, swung his arms in a march across a sitting room and stamped to a halt by the suite door. He opened it, went out and did an about-face with the skill of an old campaigner.

The old man came to the doorway and out, halting with "Now just a minute . . ."

"SAH?"

Drawing himself up, the old man made his face even more haughty. He said, "Carry on, Captain."

Apple flung up another rigorous salute. He threw it down like ridding himself of a leech, performed a quarter turn, set off marching. When he looked back while turning at the stairhead, the old man was still standing at attention.

THREE

At first he thought he had been knocked out. There was
this pain in his head. Also he realised, as he continued to
float below total awareness, that he was lying doubled up
on the back seat of a car.

I am hiding here to recover, Apple thought with hope
flapping its tatty wings. I was tailing a mysterious person
down dark alleys and sinister byways, where I got drawn
into an ambush. It wasn't easy, being outnumbered, but I
gave as good as I took and then got a crack on the skull
from behind. I have been brawling.

Coming awake suddenly, Apple remembered he had
been drunk. He saw that he was curled up in Ethel and
understood what had happened. His intention had been
to take a ten-minute break here and then go back to the
party at Lady Barre's, to see who, if anyone, looked
guilty about that little shove over the balcony. He had
fallen asleep.

With a hand held on the top of his head, just in case the
nail sticking in there was real, not imaginary, Apple told
himself he might still have time, the party might still be
going on, though there was something about the grey-
ness outdoors that gave him doubts.

He sat up to look at his watch, which told the rest. It
was dawn. He had been here all night.

Now Apple realised he was chilled. Shivering obedi-
ently he crept out of the back and into the driver's seat.
Doors he opened and closed delicately. Ethel was cold,

disdainful. She came alive only after he had given her six bursts of the starter and she took for ever to warm up. Apple drove off through the grim early streets. Everything was drenched with dew. The few pedestrians abroad looked suicidal or moronic or criminal.

A hovelesque snack-bar appeared. Apple parked and went in. There was comfort to be drawn from the steamy warmth, the smell of coffee and old clothes, and especially from the wary attitudes of the half-dozen silent male customers who looked moronically criminal but with no hint of suicide.

Apple caught sight of himself in a mirror. He was delighted to see that he had a jaded appearance. He was a hell-raiser toughie who had just left a wild scene, man. His eyes were red, his hair was impersonating a raped bird's nest, his tie was askew and he had a stubble of beard.

With a slight swagger of which he was unaware Apple went to the counter. Its occupier, a huge man with a face like a discarded boxing-glove, took kindly to the order of coffee and double-bacon sandwich.

Apple adopted a hell-raiser lean. His headache was already fading and he fed his improving spirits with the reminder that it was ninety per cent certain now that something ichthyological was going on with Blushers Anonymous. The push over the balcony rail said so. It could, yes, have been done by that wretched sunglasses woman, but it wasn't likely. And there again, if she was a genuine blusher, how come she was so pushy?

Aloud, Apple said, "No pun intended."

Boxing-glove asked from the griddle, "What say, mate?"

Casually, Apple told him to make that sandwich a triple. This verbal recovery and his largesse with himself and the ninety per cent certainty combined to have him refrain from recalling how he had made testicles of his pro-Communist gambit at the party.

His breakfast came. While munching with medium gusto through the inch-thick slabs of bread, Apple managed to get two more views of himself in the mirror. Whenever the other customers seemed to be in danger of taking him for granted, he stretched one arm or gave a low chuckle.

Finished, plate crumbless, Apple created a faint rake limp in walking to the door. He would have thrown something cryptic back at Boxing-glove except for knowing the man might ask him what he was talking about. The best exiter he could come up with was another chuckle, though it was considerably lower than the others.

Apple collected Ethel and headed for home. He wished he had the guts to show up at the United Kingdom Philological Institute in his present state. But guts apart he had to rest, be fresh for the afternoon. He was almost sure that he perhaps intended telling Angus Watkin of his BA suspicions, maybe.

Apple yawned. He was beginning to feel putrid. That's what hangovers were all about, he insisted to himself. He refused to blame his worsening condition on the breakfast of fried food, grease, white bread and caffeine. Such considerations he had long ago given up, which gutsy abstinence had afforded him a great deal of pride.

At home Apple got into a hot bath. Finishing off with a shower that was a shade less hot in order to seem cold, he set about the task of shaving. He gave up on the first cut.

The telephone rang. With a piece of paper stuck on his wound to stop the bleeding, Apple went to answer. The caller was Jennifer Rolph.

She said, "I hope I didn't wake you, Appleton."

"Been up since dawn," Apple said. "By the way, I'm

sorry for leaving the bash last night without saying my good-nights and thank-yous."

"Did you? I didn't notice and I doubt if anyone else did. Everybody got rather sloshed. Except me, due to work. I'm run off my feet."

"Blushers Anonymous?"

"Right. People're joining thick and fast. You'll see lots of new faces at tonight's meeting. I'm on my seventh notebook. Which brings me to the purpose of this call."

"You want to make me president of BA," Apple said. He found he had no trouble in picturing Jennifer, with her eyes of Lincoln green. "Thank you."

She laughed. "No, but there seems to be some confusion over your biographical details. Lady B noticed it yesterday."

"What's the problem, Jen?"

"I have you down as being a philologist, and the other night you said you were a scientist. But perhaps you're both."

"In a way," Apple said carefully. "It's a little difficult to explain."

Jennifer said, "Perhaps we could have a quiet moment together sometime and you could try explaining."

"As a matter of fact, Lady B was saying at the party that she wants to do that."

"Yes? She hasn't mentioned it. Should I jog her elbow, fix an appointment?"

"Not yet," Apple said, still walking his words with care. "There's plenty of time."

"Okay," Jennifer said. "Until tonight, then."

After disconnecting Apple headed for his bedroom. He swung around and went back as the telephone rang again. This time the caller was an unknown female with a voice that throbbed its competence. She addressed Apple by a series of numbers and said that today's gathering at Bigelow Titles had been cancelled due to sickness.

"How about tomorrow's?"

"You will be informed." The line died.

The news of cancellation convincing Apple that he had been determined to tell the whole BA thing to Angus Watkin, he shook his fist at air in aggravation.

Stamping to the bedroom he wondered if he ought to call Jennifer back and ask her to fix an appointment with Lady Barre. He decided not, since he would be seeing them both tonight. As well as Wendy.

Apple went back to the telephone. When connected he said, "Sorry I didn't get a chance to talk to you last night."

"Same here," Wendy said. "But it was a fun party."

"Did you escape from that nuisance?"

"I pointed you out to him and said you were my boyfriend, which seemed to do the trick, even though you weren't much in evidence after that."

"I left early. Headache."

Wendy said, "Whenever I use that story it means I was well sozzled."

They both laughed. Apple said, "How about if I pick you up earlyish this evening. We could have a snack or whatever and then go on to the meeting."

"Lovely idea, Appleton. It's a date."

It wasn't until he was getting into bed a minute later, oblivion the plan, that Apple realised with a swoop of guilt that he hadn't given one single worried thought to the question of Ethel's legitimacy. He pulled the covers over his head.

Apple went downstairs at Harlequin Mansions humming. He was shaved, he wore casual slacks and windcheater, he earlier had gone to an exclusive Mayfair garage where a mechanic with clean hands and a ciga-rette-holder had given Ethel a slow, sensuous greasing.

Outside, Apple set off to the underground car park. Street lamps were on although dusk was a rumour as yet. It was Apple's favourite time of day, when all things wax mellow. He was breathing in the evening ambience along with autumn's tang when he noticed the man.

He was ten metres ahead, leaning against a car, the pose so casual that it had to be acted. This in addition to the fact that he was definitely spook material—right height, bland of dress and style, aged about thirty.

Spooky could be there for any one of a dozen reasons related to any one of the hundreds of people who lived hereabouts, Apple knew, just as he knew that the man could possibly be an insurance salesman or a car thief. But Apple had a feeling.

He stopped, looked at his watch without noting the time, made a complete turn, started back the other way. That was when he saw the other man.

This one bore the same stamp as the first. Sole differ-ence was in number of years, forty here, and a more mature lean. He sagged against the wall as though they had gone to school together.

Apple looked behind. Spooky was coming, he was un-surprised to see. He turned back and stopped. The other man straightened from the wall as if having just discov-ered that it had stolen his marbles.

Apple was between building and parked cars. Moving to the latter, to the front of a long-nosed Jaguar, he threw himself into a stylish vault. No sooner were his hands on the Jag's nose than they were off again and he was land-ing in the roadway with feet neat.

The vault would have been formidable for a man of normal height; for Apple, it was a piece of cake made in Vienna. That there was ample space to allow walking through between the Jaguar and the next car Apple declined to acknowledge.

He began to go on in the same direction. Ten steps and he was level with Old Hand, who, expressionless, turned and started to move along abreast on his own side of the vehicular barrier. Apple looked back.

Spooky had just come through to the road in front of the Jaguar. Although he pulled up short, he was unable to avoid being bumped by a youth on a bicycle. This knocked him back between the cars.

After checking on his own forward progress, less out of concern for safety than from a fear of becoming similarly involved in farce, Apple looked back again.

Spooky came back onto the roadway and started to run. Almost at once he reached the cyclist (who shot up a protective arm), passed him and drew on. His face was as grim as only hate or the suspicion of ridicule can create.

Apple also set off running. He was not about to tangle outnumberedly with angry operatives, whoever they might be, and they might be anybody.

At the other side of the parked cars, Old Hand was keeping abreast at a lope. Spooky was coming along strongly behind. Apple, who had been given athletic training in addition to owning stilty legs, decided to give the boys a bit of exercise. He put on speed.

There was a four-way junction. Apple went back onto the pavement as he made a right turn, skimming within a metre of Old Hand, whose mouth was open and whose cheeks were trembling. Apple ran on.

Looking back at the next corner he saw that both men were pounding along side by side. Neither looked happy. He slowed to stop them from getting too disheartened, quitting. That he didn't give them a wave of encouragement was because that, he felt, would have been offensive.

After one full circle of the block and then a straight-off, Apple was approaching where the British Museum stood back like a grimy blockhouse behind its railings.

Soon, Apple thought, he would be at busy Tottenham Court Road and able to find a cab, since going back for Ethel was obviously not on the menu. So now was the time for Hare to say good-bye to hounds.

In crossing the roadway, Apple paused to pick up a discarded newspaper. He rolled it as he bounded on, rapidly increasing his speed. By the time he reached the British Museum area he was racing. He liked his style. Grinning, he stuck out his arm and held the newspaper against the rails so that it went clap-clap-clap.

Leaving the taxi two streets away, Apple headed for Wendy's place at a thrusting stride. He was a man who liked to be prompt and it looked as though he would be a minute and a half late, but he didn't want to run again because that would mean arriving in a fluster and he was trying to present a suave image.

Apple came to the tall house, went up the steps and into a hall. On the right was a flight of stairs, which, as per Wendy's instructions, he climbed. The first door on the first landing was the one. He knocked.

There was no answer, although the door's trembly response to his knock showed that it was unlatched, ready for a caller. Apple would have assumed Wendy to be in the bathroom except for remembering her saying that it was a communal deal, along the landing. So, he told himself uneasily, that's where she could be. He waited.

After one minute a door farther along opened, a wet-haired man in a robe came out and then went around a corner. The bathroom theory seemed dead.

Not at all liking that thought's phrasing, Apple

knocked again and called an hello. Still no answer. Using a forefinger he poked the door open, creating barely an inch of space. He peeked inside. What he saw made him push the door open wide with a slam. The squeal of hinges matched the way his hair seemed to stand on end.

The room was a manic mess. The floor was a jumble of sheets and blankets, clothing, framed pictures with their backs loose, papers, cooking utensils, books wantonly spreadeagled.

A naked mattress stood propped against the wall, a wide-open wardrobe's contents were avalanched out. Every cupboard of the corner kitchenette had been denuded and every container therefrom had been emptied onto the existing chaos, garnishing with sugar, flour, preserves and corn flakes.

Apple felt pale. "Wendy?" he said, for some reason using a whisper. He repeated the name as he high-stepped here and there, looking in likely places for the room's owner. It didn't take long. She was absent.

It took longer to find the telephone, which Apple tensely set about doing after he had pushed the door closed. Why his search was lengthy was due to his wish to do as little disturbing as possible.

Instrument discovered on the floor, under a cushion, Apple dialled Upstairs. A male voice which had become familiar lately answered. Apple, identification formality over with, said, "I want an expert, please."

"Somehow, that doesn't surprise me."

"Search. At once."

Following a pause the duty officer asked, "Not Documents?"

Politely: "No, thank you."

"Wounds, mayhap?"

"Just Search, thanks. It's urgent."

"We're certainly busy of late," the man said, dry as old

toast. "Location and number." When these had been given he closed out with "Call you back."

Apple put the hand-set down. Rising from his crouch he let his eyes wander over the vaguely pornographic anarchy. There was, he agreed, the possibility that this was the work of a common burglar. But where was Wendy?

It occurred to Apple with a grade-three tingling on his neck that Wendy, in fact, could have gone to get the police, preferring not to touch even the telephone.

It rang. Apple stooped to pick up the receiver. The duty officer said, "He'll be there soonest. Call him Pockets. He's short, fat and fifty. I wouldn't dream of asking what's going on." The line clicked off.

When Apple had stopped sympathising with the duty officer, he told himself that, if burglary was out, what was going on could be connected with Old Hand and Spooky. But how?

There was a squealing sound. It took Apple into a turn, one hand smoothing down his hair. The door was ending its opening sweep. In the doorway stood a woman, a stranger. Her facial expression was a mistake.

Apple said, "Hello."

The woman stared. She was thickset, sturdy as a man in her denim jeans and jacket. About forty, hair in a crew-cut, she had the features that cartoonists matched with tall pointed hats, slinky black cats and flying broomsticks. This warty face was trying to smile.

She asked, "What's going on here?"

Apple asked, "Who are you?"

The woman asked, "Who are *you?*"

"I'm a friend of Miss—er—of Wendy's."

"I see. You don't know your friend's last name."

"Of course I do," Apple lied as if amused. "But I just realised there's no reason I should give it to you."

Smile given up on, face improved to straightforward ugly, the woman said, "I'm the landlady."

"Hello again."

"Where's Wendy?"

"I have no idea," Apple said.

"Did you do this?"

"Certainly not. I only got here a couple of minutes ago."

The woman came inside, close to Apple, the while looking up at him suspiciously in physical semi-profile as though ready to fling herself away if he made a sudden move.

She asked, "Did you see who did it?"

"Sorry."

"So why are you hanging around?"

"Thought I might do a bit of tidying," Apple again lied. He bent toward the mess. "If you'll excuse me."

Although he saw the blow coming he was unable to make a defensive movement. The woman was too fast, too skilled. She swung the right-hander like a seasoned middleweight, putting her whole torso into the act.

The punch caught Apple on the side of his jaw. He saw red lights, felt blue pain, heard black drums. Not completely rendered unconscious, he was aware of falling. It seemed a long way down. He wondered if he would land on a balcony and need to play soldier. His body was so tense in expectancy of a cruel landing that when he finally settled into softness it came as a shock. He groaned.

Apple went on groaning softly, soothed by the sound, as his mind drifted about like an ambitious feather. He knew where he was, in Wendy's bed-sitter, just as surely as he knew he was floating down a river on a raft.

The drift came to an end and Apple stopped groaning. He missed it. Conscious, examining the ceiling cracks, he rubbed his chin. It was as tender as his sensibilities, his discomfort inside at having fallen for that old gag of the attacker pretending to be wary of attack, thus being midway into the stance for attacking.

He sat up. The lady road-driller had gone, the door was closed, the room had been given a rough tidying. Apple got the impression that the job had been unfinished, that the woman had been interrupted, or driven off by his groans and imminent consciousness.

But what the Biblical-sense was it all about?—he wondered, though not unhappily.

He cocked his head at a new sound. It was a whistling and it came from the landing. The tune was an old music-hall refrain, "I was Born Upstairs in a Workhouse." Apple stepped to the door and drew it open.

The man arriving at the stairhead was short, fat and fifty. He wore a cap and a raincoat, these dun browns separated by a face of cheery pink.

Apple said, "Hello, Pockets."

Breaking off his whistle the man said, "Yes, I've heard of you. Speakfreak, right?"

"That's it. Call me Apple. Come in."

Door closed, Apple explained about the partial tidying. He left Witch-face out of it, partly because of need-to-know, partly because he was keeping the cards of this game close to his chest. "It happened when I slipped out to call in, ask for you."

"What is it you want to know? Who made the search or who did the tidy?"

"I want to know anything you can tell me."

Bending, Pockets began to nose about like a scavenger at the city dump. He said, "I think we're due for a bit of rain."

"Yes," Apple said impatiently. "There aren't many signs left for you to read, I'm afraid."

"Oh, you'd be surprised. The German way with neatness, the way a Frenchman handles lingerie, the general training. There's always a hint or two about."

"It might have been a straight burglary."

Pockets shook his head while looking under a book. "Doubt that. Most burglars are sexually twisted, not criminal in the social sense. Their major act is of illicit entry, the fact of penetration. Next they like to use the place as a bathroom. A table or a bed or the middle of a carpet. Real sick."

"That's a new one on me."

"It's not talked about. Most burglary victims're so disgusted, even ashamed in some obscure and disturbing way, that they clean up and fail to mention it to the coppers. Often they don't even tell their friends."

"So we haven't had a burglar here."

"We haven't."

"Have we had a spook?"

"No question of that, looks like," Pockets said. "Hold your horses a bit." Humming snatches of "Don't Go Down the Mine, Dad," he continued to search around. At length, straightening, face pinker than ever, he said, "Difficult, of course, under the circs, but I can tell you that it wasn't the work of an Anglo-Saxon, and it was probably done by either a Russian, a Slav or an Israeli."

Apple vacated the room three minutes after Pockets left, drawing the door into its frame. He had a niggle about not doing at least a partial tidy, but Wendy came first. That he didn't feel even more urgent as to her whereabouts stemmed from his admission that her absence could be innocent. Among other possibilities, she could have been harmlessly lured away in chase of a wild goose so that the search could take place.

Further along on the same floor Apple knocked on a

door. A voice with an accent which Apple placed as being from an area some twenty miles south of Dublin called from within, "If you didn't get the milk, go away."

"Excuse me," Apple said. "Do you know Wendy Harper from down the hall?" The name he had found on a letter.

After a pause: "Only to nod at."

"Never mind. Where can I find the landlady, please?"

The voice said, "Landlord. The basement flat. Do you always shout like a lunatic?"

"Sorry about that."

"Listen. You wouldn't happen to have a bottle of milk about you, would you?"

"Afraid not," Apple said. "You wouldn't happen to have heard a disturbance recently from Wendy's part, would you?"

"I'm not the nosy type," the voice said. "Good-bye."

Jogging down two flights of stairs, meanwhile agreeing with himself that London was full of peculiar people, Apple came to a lurky door with a sign saying that all complaints had to be delivered by letter. He rapped.

The man who opened up was small, thin and plaintive, like one line of doggerel. Without taking the pipe out of his mouth he talked spittily about that bloody dog next door and his cousin who won the football pools last month.

"Me, I get noisy dogs," he said. "Who?"

"Wendy Harper. Number four."

"She's a sub-let, which is real nice of me. Only seen her twice. Stand-offish."

"Shy," Apple said. "So you don't know where I could find her if she's not home."

"No, I don't."

After hearing about the dirty stuff they shoved at you

on the telly nowadays and why Winston Churchill was nobody's fool, Apple got away.

The next move was obvious, he thought. It was one that ought to be made even if Wendy suddenly appeared, coming back smiling from somewhere innocent, perhaps a trip to the grocery store.

Out in the street, telling himself defensively that people couldn't very well go around with bottles of milk in their pockets, Apple set off walking at a rapid stride.

Above the glum street lighting the sky was dark. Apple wished he could see himself from up there, a high shot of the secret agent stalking the fetid streets of slumland; this while he was busy being logical about the situation.

If Wendy wasn't shopping, detained somewhere in the rush-hour, or standing in a queue at the police station to report her robbery, Apple queried, where was she? Since she had been waiting outside for the cottage date, it would seem that she was the prompt and reliable type. So, if an innocent absence was ruled out, she must be either injured, dead, a prisoner, or in hot pursuit of the thieves. Except that the last didn't seem to account for the mysterious Witch-face.

On the corner stood a pub. Apple went in. Above the thinnish early crowd he saw a telephone booth, crossed to it while sagging at the knees and stepped inside. Door footed ajar, he dialled Upstairs. He asked, when the same duty officer answered, "Don't you ever go home?"

The man said, "We're running out of experts here."

Ignoring that Apple gave a series of numbers. They identified the man he wished to contact. In a less brash tone the duty officer said, "Give me ten minutes."

Apple sagged out and over to the bar. He got served with a mineral water, which might have been the reason two nearby men edged away, Apple was generously will-

ing to acknowledge, though he felt that in all probability
it was because he was giving out the hunter's aura of
viciousness and power.

After eleven and a half minutes Apple returned to the
booth. He got through to the duty officer, who asked,
"Can this wait?"

In the indolent manner that he felt would be the most
impressive, Apple said, "Myself I'm rather inclined to
think it's a tiny bit urgent."

"In that case God will oblige."

It was a large pet shop. Through the entrance, Apple
sidled guiltily past cages. Most of them held those sweet
snuffly little puppies that people buy only to find out
they're female kittens. There was a smell of sawdust and
stale nurses.

Next came a foodstuffs room, shelves holding canned
and packaged goods. Leaning at one side was a short,
badly worn man in a blue boiler suit and running shoes
that had given up trying to be white.

Apple stopped. "The ubiquitous Albert," he said.

The older man, Angus Watkin's assistant/bodyguard/
driver, said in a Cockney grind, "Don't know if I care for
the sound of that."

Cheerfully: "Good."

"We're full of piss and acid tonight, aren't we?"

"As always. Now would you please get on with it. I
don't have all the time in the world."

"Take me to your leader—that's what you're supposed
to say. You don't know nothing."

Apple asked, "Is it far from here?"

"A pebble's throw," Albert said. "Right through that
doorway." He pointed. "And mind your nut. It's only
three yards high." He sniggered.

Crossing the room, Apple told Albert in Magyar that

he was a witless, graceless midget with the face of a chewed cabbage. He would have used English except for Albert being one of those unarmed-combat specialists who can break your arm with a blink.

The short man was muttering, a scowl in his voice, as Apple passed through the doorway. He came into a skylighted area. It was intended to look like a jungle glade. The plastic palm trees stood there as realistically as galley-slaves in party hats.

On raffia turf beside the tin pond lay a log made out of fibreglass. On the log sat Angus Watkin. He held a slice of bread, from which he was separating bits to throw down to the pond's goldfish.

Apple cleared his throat like a butler. Without looking around Watkin said, "Don't hover on the sidelines, Porter. Come and sit down."

Since sharing the short log with his Control would be overly familiar, Apple thought, instead of viewing it as unappealing, which would have been ill-mannered, he lowered himself into a cross-legged sit on the turf.

He said, "Goldfish have a memory span of only three seconds, I understand."

Lazily, Angus Watkin said, "One hopes that one wasn't dragged here at panic notice to be given one of your little gems, Porter, or even two."

"No, sir. Just thought I'd mention it."

"And having made said mention, you will of course now rush without further preamble into the reason for this urgent emergency meeting. Mmm?"

"Yes, sir."

"I am, I confess," Angus Watkin said, "burning to know what in all creation could have provoked you into making this unusual move. Obviously, the matter is of great consequence."

Apple had the curious sensation that he was shrinking. Even his voice sounded small for "Obviously, sir."

"Pray begin, Porter."

The shrinking process Apple ended by coming out of his cringe. Back straight, he was astounded to hear himself say, voice firm, "It's about Ethel, sir." He almost cringed again.

It seemed to take Angus Watkin five minutes to separate a pinch of bread from his slice and toss it into the water, grandly, like an earl gifting his doxy with a bauble. He then turned to Apple and said blandly, "I beg your pardon?"

"My car," Apple said with a kind of gallant desperation, his chin out and his eyes meek. "Ex-London taxicab. Given the name of Ethel while in service with various departments of police espionage, including Upstairs. I believe, sir, that you are not unaware of Ethel's existence."

With a hint of resignation: "That is so."

His astonishment gone, but not forgotten, Apple told the whole story, from Stanley Field and the Antique London Taxicab Owners Guild to the discovery of the log-book's phoniness. He ended, "That was quite a shock."

"No doubt it was, Porter," Angus Watkin said. "But how does this rending tragedy relate to what it is that you wish so urgently to see me about?"

"And when I got over the shock," Apple said with the fused hearing-aid act he had learned from Watkin himself, "I could see that the problem wasn't really so bad. All I needed was a new forgery."

His Control tossed down another bauble, which, the weight of his arm suggested, might be made of lead. He said, "Get to the urgency, if you please."

"Yes, sir. Right away, sir. I simply wanted to point out

that things sometimes are not what they seem. Things good, bad or indifferent."

Angus Watkin said in a near drawl, "I never suspected you of profundity, Porter. *Things sometimes are not what they seem.* Well well."

"Yes, sir," Apple said unhappily.

"Do you know what I have often thought when waxing deep?"

"No, sir."

Watkin said, "That there's good and bad in everyone."

Apple offered space a weak smile as well as a frown in the hopes of stating thereby that he didn't mind his chief having a little joke at his expense, or, should Watkin be serious, that the statement was most interesting, or, if Watkin was testing him for idiocy, that he had known it all along, or, in case Watkin was hoping to insult him, that he was insulted.

"But enough of this merry chatter," Angus Watkin said. "The urgency, Porter. Get on with it."

Apple twitched his shoulders straight, the condemned man about to climb the thirteen steps. He said, tone formal, "I have been doing some investigating."

"Of what, precisely?"

"Of an organization which might be attempting to undermine the security of this nation."

"But it doesn't seem so, of course. Things sometimes being the way they are, as we know."

Fuse gone again: "Having my suspicions, I attempted to infiltrate the organization. At last I succeeded. My suspicions grew. I have been brutally assaulted twice, followed, thrown off a high balcony. Two men tried to corner me in the street this evening, and now a person has gone missing under extremely peculiar circumstances."

Angus Watkin looked at him. "One imagines that this is connected with your requests for experts."

Apple told himself he ought to have known that God Watkin would find out. "Exactly, sir," he said briskly, all business. "They were not for personal reasons, naturally. Not in the slightest. Oh no."

"Tell me, Porter, what is this organization?"

Quietly: "It's something recent."

"The name, please."

Grimly: "Blushers Anonymous."

With no change in face or manner, Angus Watkin threw the whole slice of bread into the pond. From the splash, drops of water flew. One landed on Apple's cheek. He allowed it to live unwiped and trickle down to his chin because he felt that way.

"Did I hear you right, Porter?"

"You did, sir."

"Blushers Anonymous."

"Yes, sir."

Angus Watkin closed his eyes on a sigh, like a father running out of fondness. "I suppose you had better tell me all about it."

Apple, shuffling himself one inch closer, obliged. The telling didn't take up much time. Even though he added frills, offered sections of dialogue and went so far as to describe Spooky and Old Hand, the story declined to be made long. Worse, the evidence of a plot sounded not so much weak as withered.

Angus Watkin opened his eyes. Looking down at the fishes he said, "The scheme as you see it being, I assume, to make contact with persons who are sensitive and therefore vulnerable in respect of manipulation."

"Exactly, sir. I couldn't have phrased it better."

"Well, in the first place, Porter, if such a scheme were

actually underway it would be none of our business. There are other people to take care of these matters."

"But—"

"In the second place, there is the premise on character. It does not necessarily follow that if a person is sensitive he is vulnerable."

"I wouldn't go so far as to say that, sir."

"It isn't you who's saying it."

"That's true, sir."

"But let me put it another way, Porter," Angus Watkin said. "Are you yourself vulnerable?"

"I, sir?" Apple said, patting himself. "No, sir. Not in the least."

"You are, however, a blusher of some consequence. And your point is that blushers are sensitive."

Apple opened his mouth to answer, could think of no answer, closed his mouth, realised he could say he had been cured, opened his mouth to say it and decided he couldn't get away with the lie. He closed his mouth.

". . . could have been a common mugger, or a hoodlum mistaking you for someone else," Angus Watkin was saying. "The balcony incident could have been due to somebody who was just as drunk as you undoubtedly were bumping against you. The two men this evening, that could be explained in so many ways it's hardly worth going into. The same with the absence of this female, who, I'll wager, is young and attractive. Wager won, Porter?"

"It all depends what you mean by attractive, sir."

"Try not to talk like a fool."

"Sorry," Apple said. "But what about the woman who knocked me out, nearly?"

Angus Watkin offered, "A lunatic on the loose? The original thief come back to finish the job? Or to remove some clue she had left behind? A friend of your friend's who was being protective, taking *you* for the thief? A victim-type who thought you were about to attack her?"

Implacably Apple said, "She claimed to be the landlady. It wasn't true. And Pockets said—"

"People lie and experts make mistakes," Angus Watkin cut in. He rose with an unmistakable air of finality, like an actor lifting his voice for his exit-line. He circled the pond. "I wouldn't dream of thinking you merely wanted help in finding this missing female, Porter. Not consciously wanted. Passion does have a way of unbalancing some of us."

"It isn't that at all, sir."

Watkin turned by the doorway. He said, "My advice is for you to go home, have a nice soothing cup of tea, and wait for the lady to telephone with an apology for being delayed at the hairdresser's, where she had gone when half-way through a complete reorganization of her room, back to which she finishingly sent a karate-instructor friend, with whom she is having a romantic relationship, and who is fiercely jealous, particularly of men who resemble the lady's father, who was an obsessively tidy, gangly, blind-in-love, melodramatic, inebriated nincompoop." He left the glade.

Apple began to sag when he had passed the British Museum, as though the weight of its culture had come out and climbed on his back. By the time he was within distant sight of Harlequin Mansions he was less than six feet tall, bent at knee, hip and neck. Stares of curious pedestrians he returned with generous interest, causing the starers to hurry on or to touch their clothing.

The street ahead was clean. Apple could see nobody anywhere who looked familiar or who roused his suspicion. He knew, however, that the enemy could be waiting in a car or watching from a window or other vantage point.

Once out of sight in the back alley, Apple straightened. It was pleasant. Two peaceful minutes it took him to climb the service stairs in Harlequin Mansions and enter his flat. The peace was over.

Apple paced a circle around the living room. He craved the comfort of a cup of tea but because tea was what the odious Watkin had prescribed, he refused to indulge. It was bad enough that he had actually come here, as also per God's advice, instead of doing something positive.

Not knowing what he meant, what he could have done that was positive or anything else, Apple left the matter there and strode to the kitchen. Following a triumphant sneer at the kettle, he went back to the main room.

He paced. His jaw when he touched it offered neither pain nor swelling, the lump on the back of his head had gone without a trace. He paced.

Apple teetered on a curve when acknowledging that as well as odious, Angus Watkin was wily, and only on rare occasions did he become directly offensive, as had happened this evening. Therefore, were those departing insults offered in order to goad his underling into further efforts, to try hard for success so as to be able to say to his chief, I told you so? True, a Blushers Anonymous plot might not be within Watkin's jurisdiction, but that didn't mean he wouldn't want to be in on it one way or another. There was nothing he didn't want to be in on.

Apple stopped pacing. As he did, the telephone rang. Three strides took him into the corner. Lifting the receiver he heard, "Hello, Appleton."

He snapped, "Wendy?"

"Yes."

He allowed his belly to balloon with relief, despite the

vague essence of threat in his, "If you've been to the hairdresser's . . ."

"What d'you mean?" Her voice was tense.

"Nothing, nothing. You're all right?"

"Yes."

"At home?"

"No. Did you go there?"

"Yes," Apple said. "I wonder if you know what I found."

"Never mind that now," Wendy said. "Look, Appleton, can you come to get me?"

"Why yes. Of course. I don't understand."

"I'll explain later. I'm a bit shaken. And I have no money with me for a taxi or a bus or anything."

"I'm on my way," Apple said. "Where are you?"

She told him, adding, "There's no violent hurry, so please don't go and have an accident."

"As long as you're okay."

"I'm perfectly fine, just a bit shattered. Really."

"Half an hour at the most. Hold on."

"This is good of you, Appleton."

"See you soon," Apple said. He cradled the receiver, left the room. He felt glad, resolute, hopeful. After checking his pockets to make sure he had cab fare (it would be injudicious to go to get Ethel from the garage, where enemies could be waiting) he let himself out of the flat.

Inside, the telephone rang. Apple fumbled out his key, got inside and hurried to the living room while pretending he was taking his time. The ringing didn't stop and the caller was Angus Watkin.

Apple was unaware of straightening with his "Yes, sir?"

"I trust you enjoyed your tea, Porter."

Despising himself: "I did, sir, yes."

"But to the nub," Watkin said. "Having put out a little feeler, I now have an explanation for your brush with a pair of desperadoes in the street this evening."

"That's interesting," Apple said, hoping for the worst, for them not to have been something sane and respectable.

"They were Special Branch officers. And they were attempting to question you."

"Question *me?*"

Angus Watkin said, "It seems that at a meeting of your Blushers Anonymous an unusually tall man was talking about his job as a scientist in what was described to the Special Branch, by a person who was at the meeting, as a provocative manner."

"I don't get that," Apple lied.

"In other words, the tall man seemed to be hoping to attract interest of a subversive nature."

"That finky person was misreading my attitude."

Angus Watkin said, "And possibly you didn't say you were a scientist, Porter."

"Yes, I did. I am. Philology is a science."

"Curiously enough, I did suggest that in a certain quarter, while at the same time explaining that you posed no threat to national security. You will not, I believe, be troubled again by street desperadoes."

"Thank you, sir."

"You sound somewhat agitated, Porter."

"I was just on my way out, to go and meet Wendy. That's the ex-missing lady."

"Who telephoned you, of course."

Apple almost growled in saying, "She's in some kind of trouble, I think."

"Couldn't pay the hairdresser?" Angus Watkin submitted. "But apart from that, and the recognition that how you spend your free time is entirely your own affair, I would like to refer to the vehicle which you own."

As though to hear better, Apple curved himself into a crouch. He asked, "Ethel, sir?"

"That same. It will be arranged at once for documents to be created. Forged, some might crudely say."

"Did I hear you say . . . ?"

"Yes, Porter. You will be supplied with a log-book of the finest craftsmanship, suitably aged."

Smiling, standing straight again in delight, Apple fumbled out his thanks. He said, "You have no idea what this will mean to me, sir."

"I am not doing this for you," Angus Watkin said. "I am doing it for Ethel."

"Yes, sir," Apple said with the right amount of professional, sentimentless snap.

"She deserves it in her declining years."

"I couldn't agree more, sir."

Watkin said, "And as to that, the subject of age, you will need to call in and supply the date of birth." He paused. "Any date you wish." The line went dead.

Thoughtless, Apple hurried out of the flat, went down to the street and ran along to the garage. He didn't start to think until he and Ethel were out and rolling. Then, from trying to give his mind to too many things at the same time, he became confused.

He was thinking about getting as swiftly as possible to Wendy, waiting in a shattered state in Maida Vale.

He was holding to the probability that Wendy had been, and perhaps still was, in some kind of danger, into which he himself might be drawn.

He was wondering who could have been the BA member who finked to the Special Branch.

He was telling himself that Angus Watkin's remark relating to free time could only mean a green light, which would be on account of he believed Blushers Anonymous might not be so innocent after all, as, it seemed, did the Special Branch.

He was dwelling on the marvellous fact that Ethel was going to get immaculate papers.

He was considering that the granting of those papers could be another way of Watkin's of giving the go-ahead —for what other reason could there be for this sudden change of mind?

Meanwhile, underneath his various cogitations, Apple was thinking with a tingle that he could give Ethel any birthdate he wanted, which was honey, since in the snobby antique-automobile world age was synonymous with pedigree. Every month counted like a noble ancestor. He could make Ethel much older. He could give her an extra *two years.*

As he allowed the birthdate thought to surface, superseding all others, Apple shivered. His hairline moved. He felt excited. A sensation went through him which he gratefully recognised as cynicism.

Apple pictured himself doing it, telling a lie on the telephone when he called in, his mouth in a wry lift at one corner. He saw Ethel thereafter receiving extra deference; saw her owner forever sticking to the lie; saw him develop in his secret career into a hard, crafty, pro operative.

Lying would be the right move, Apple knew. Not only did he himself want this for Ethel, Angus Watkin wanted it as well. *Any date you wish,* he had said, which, the way it was put, could only be an encouragement to be devious.

Apple's excitement would have grown if it hadn't been for two other sensations. Nor was it simply that they intruded; they fought each other like a couple over the affections of a lapdog. One was discomfort at his reasoning, the other nausea stemming from his suspicion that he was going to do the Right Thing.

He needed to act on the matter right away, Apple accepted. At once. Delay would be fatal.

An agonizing three minutes passed before Apple saw a place to park on the commercial road. He slammed to a stop, leapt out of Ethel, locked up in a clatter of metal and set off to find a telephone. When he spotted a street booth he went stalking toward it as though it owed him money.

Inside, he dialled Upstairs and gabbled through the preliminaries. A cool female asked if she could be of service. Apple said, "I'm going to give a date to you to be passed on to Documents. Listen, please." He listened himself. He was saddened to hear his voice pronounce the true date.

Grubbily, Apple mused that Wendy will have been to see a sick aunt, who kept her there talking for hours, until Wendy was absolutely shattered. That free-time remark of Watkin's merely meant that the underling was going to have much more of it as far as working for Upstairs was concerned. Angus Watkin believed there was something sinister about Blushers Anonymous the way Germans don't like sausage. Ethel was being given new documents because Upstairs had decided she might be usefully employed again one of these days.

The counter-attack didn't last long. For a while after his treachery to himself back there on the telephone it was an easement. But it faded.

Apple told himself in any case that the fact of Ethel getting fresh papers was great enough in itself, without wishing for more. He was cheerful again by the time, watching street nameplates, he turned the last corner in Maida Vale.

It was one of those brooding, broad, tree-laden avenues that always look damp, as if they want to be rivers. Houses were mostly hidden behind walls or more trees. The few parked cars present had the jaded air of having been abandoned after the getaway.

Apple slowed to a sub-walk crawl, his headlights full on. There was no sign of life. Wendy had said she would be waiting here, so was he supposed to blow the horn, shout? Or could an enemy be using Wendy as bait for a trap?

Forget the melodrama, Apple thought. He picked up speed to a canter, straddling the white line not so much by way of caution but because it felt illicit.

Soon, from behind one of the trees that lined the kerbs, trees whose shadows were slinking back behind Ethel into the darkness like spies, a face appeared.

Apple speeded up and then came to a fast halt. He got out as Wendy stepped fully clear of her tree and it seemed only natural for them to embrace. Apple might even have gone for a kiss if Wendy hadn't pulled back with a gasped "You're terrific, Appleton. Thanks."

Apple told himself that his comment about maidens in distress was fatuous at the same time as he was making it. But Wendy said, "I was that right enough."

"But what on earth happened?"

"It's pretty weird."

"First of all, you. Sure you're okay?"

She assured him she was fine. Outwardly she looked it, trim in black pants and a black high-neck sweater. "Don't worry."

"Not shattered anymore?"

"Only around the edges. But I do want to know what you found at my place."

Apple explained how it happened that he went in the room. As he did, he was not unaware of the scene's effectiveness: the couple talking urgently under the trees, the headlights, the idling motor, the night. What did not being a verbal smoothie matter?

"Yes yes," Wendy said. "What did you find?"

"It was a disaster area. Everything thrown about, some breakage, pictures off the walls." He went on, elaborating at first and next toning down on account of Wendy's growing expression of dismay. He ended, "Messy."

"My God. How bloody awful."

"It looked to me as though someone was searching for money or something." He daren't be too knowledgeable.

"Nothing worth searching for, including money," Wendy said, grave. "Still, the mess explains it all. I've been thinking it was a rag and this confirms it."

"What d'you mean by a rag?"

"Joke, giggle, game, sport. The apple-pie bed routine."

"Rags belong in college."

"So some of my sophomoric, so-called friends decided to have a little amusement at my expense. That has to be the answer to all this."

"The mess is too much for that," Apple said, copying the echo of uncertainty in Wendy's tone. "It couldn't be the work of friends."

"Rivals, then. I don't know. All I do know for sure is that right now I need a damn big drink."

Minutes later, after a drive that Apple enjoyed making fast and swervy, they were sitting on tall stools in a wine bar. It was pretending to be a cellar in Madrid and not doing all that well at it. Apple had a sherry on the rocks, Wendy a double port-and-lemon.

"That's one million times better," she said, lowering her glass from the second drink. "I feel human again. Being kidnapped isn't all the fun in the world."

In order not to show the strength of his professional interest, Apple merely said an encouraging, "Oh?"

"It's a crazy story. Hold everything. I was standing there at the door of my room, putting the key back in my pocket—I'd just opened up, see—when someone crept up behind me and tossed a blanket over my head."

"For God's sake."

"It was soaked in ether," Wendy said. "I didn't get the smell immediately, a matter of several seconds, I suppose, and then when I realised what it was I was starting to fold."

Apple shook his head. "Fantastic."

"But really. And the stupid thing is, I just stood there wondering about the smell and telling myself this was ridiculous, it couldn't be happening. Why didn't I struggle?"

Apple didn't know, his shrug said. "Go on."

"When I came out of the ether, I was in a kitchen. Well equipped. I'd never seen it before. There was a nice smell of gravy and brussels sprouts."

"You must've been scared stiff."

"A bit," Wendy said. "I was lying on this leatherette settee thing and I could hear people talking in another room. Three or four people. Men, I'd say. My impression is that I wasn't expected to regain consciousness for a long time yet."

"Otherwise they might have tied you?"

"I dare say. Anyway, I tried the outside door. It wasn't locked so I slipped out and started running. And that was the end of it. Talk about crazy."

As Wendy nosed into her glass, Apple looked up at the plywood beams. At some point in her tale, he felt, Wendy had started lying. It was somewhere after the part of being taken with an ether-soaked blanket, which was undoubtedly true. He wished he could tell her who he was and of his Blushers Anonymous suspicions, to see what she came back with.

Glass down, Wendy was talking of how she had thought at first the kidnapping was a criminal act, perhaps rape. Apple waited for a pause in order to ask, "Were these men foreigners or British?"

"No idea. I didn't hear words."

"All right, the house. Where is it?"

"I'd say it was about a quarter of a mile from where you found me. I simply kept on running until I came to a public telephone box."

"You'd know the house again, though."

"I doubt it," Wendy said. "It's in a long terrace where they're all pretty much alike. I was stupid not to have noticed at least the door or the curtains. Not that it matters. It all amounts to nothing. It was a rag."

She was lying again, Apple felt sure. He said, "I don't know about that, Wendy. I didn't finish telling you what happened at your room."

"Can I take any more?"

"A woman came."

"What woman?"

After giving an accurate description of Witch-face, Apple asked, "Anyone you know?"

"I don't think," Wendy said, "that I would care to know anyone who sounds so awful."

"She claimed to be the landlady and then threw a tremendous right-hander at me. I was close to being knocked out. No kidding, it was quite a punch."

Wendy stared. "Hell's bells, Appleton. We've both been put through the wringer."

"And survived," Apple said. "But how does the phony landlady fit in with a rag?"

"Well, off the top of my head, I confess I don't know."

"There has to be another reason than that for her presence in your room and her aggression. Maybe, as I said before, search was the motive for it all."

"And as I said before, there's nothing, but nothing, to search for."

Here Apple felt she was telling the truth. Carefully, he suggested, "All this could, you know, have some connexion with your work."

Wendy didn't answer until she had drained her glass and licked her top lip. "I don't see how."

"You said your job was of the sensitive variety. Right?"

"I did and it's true."

"People could be professionally interested," Apple said. "You know, industrial espionage or something. You might, for instance, have the formula for a great new product, a real money-spinner, and a rival wants it. You did mention rivals."

Wendy said, "Nice try, Appleton. It's probably with you being a scientist yourself that made you come up with that one. There's nothing so romantic about my job. Except, that is, in the boy-meets-girl department, and that's where rivals come into it. Girls."

Apple hesitated. Should he, he wondered, take a chance and tell of his suspicions about Blushers Anonymous? He could do so without blowing his cover. It could be that Wendy suspected a plot herself. Could even be she suspected that the attentive Appleton, who seemed to want to know more about her work, was in it up to his high neck.

"No," Wendy said. "Alas and alack, my job isn't in that category at all."

"No secret formulas?"

"Sorry. No plans for new bombs, chemical weapons or how to feed an army on sand."

Careful again, Apple said, "About Blushers Anonymous."

"Well, okay," Wendy said, looking at her watch. "The meeting's been on half an hour, but that's fine."

"Ah," Apple said.

"And I certainly don't feel up to facing that awful mess at home. In fact, I might not feel up to going back there at all tonight."

Apple rose from his stool. "Shall we go?"

FOUR

Once inside Meen Hall, Apple and Wendy both came to sudden stops. Both also made noises of surprise. Instead of two handfuls of people down at the front, the seating was filled to three-quarters of the way back. The crowd was three or four times as big as at the last meeting, Apple figured.

He said, "See that? Blushers Anonymous is growing by leaps and bounds."

"Yes," Wendy said. She said it in such a quiet, odd way that Apple craned to sneak a surreptitious look at her face. It had a thoughtful cast.

On the platform stood a middle-aged man. One of the newcomers from last time, wearing a cap which he had pulled so low it was like a herring-bone pate, he talked with his face totally rigid while his hands played havoc with a scarf. It was as though his theme were how to be a placid strangler.

After touching Apple on the arm, Wendy went forward. She took a seat. Standing on by the mouth of the passage, Apple looked around. He was able to pick out several people he knew, including Jasper, who was whispering to a newcomer on the second row. Lady Barre seemed to be absent.

On the back row over by the tea-urn sat Jennifer Rolph. Head lowered like a desperate student at exam time, she was writing busily, taking information from a pale teenage girl who, pulling her fingers apart, sat at her side in a matching hunch.

Waiting their turns to be enrolled by Jennifer were three other first-timers, people Apple had never seen before. Ignoring each other as thoroughly as though they were lifelong friends, they stood in a neat line.

His strangling demonstration over, the man up front glided down and into the seating. His place on the platform was taken, after Jennifer had called out a name, by a youngish woman in a safari suit and dark glasses. Holding a burp-fist in front of her mouth she began to talk.

Apple sagged against the wall comfortably. So interested did he become in the speaker's problem of blushing only when she boarded a number 28 bus, on weekdays, if it was raining, that he forgot the situation. He came back to it again as the woman stepped down.

Jennifer Rolph called a name and then went back to her notetaking. The person she was dealing with was the last newcomer, Apple saw. In a minute he strolled that way, whistling a tune in his head so he wouldn't hear what the latest speaker was saying and get involved. As it was, he knew that one of these wet days he would go out of his way to catch a 28.

Another minute and the new member left. Apple took his place beside Jennifer. "Hello, Jen."

She gave a warm smile that included her green eyes. "Hello, Appleton. Aren't I the busy bee?"

"What would we do without you."

"Manage splendidly, no doubt."

"This surge of interest is fantastic."

"It's just wonderful," Jennifer said. With the toe of her sensible shoe she tapped a red pigskin case, one of a pair, the type carried by girls in Chelsea when they want to be taken for models. "That's Files. A dozen of my notebooks crammed with information on our members."

"And the other case?"

"Lady Barre's. It's crammed with cosmetics, paperback love stories and chewing gum."

"She's a gum chewer?"

"No, but she says you never know when she might want to start. Suddenly."

They laughed in silence. Apple said, "She's quite a character, that one."

"As a popular phrase had it before I was born, you can say that again."

"I haven't seen her around this evening."

Jennifer said, "She had something to do." She raised her chin toward the front, pointing without using a hand, which Apple liked because it was old-fashioned, an Englishism which was slowly dying, like giving a woman your seat on public transport.

Apple sighed. Not for the first time, he wished his damp liberalism with its slight leftish inclination could get closer to his several conservative yearnings.

He said, "Sorry?"

Jennifer repeated her reference to the subject of her chin-point. "Wendy. I saw you come in with her. Are you two a twosome?"

"Friends," Apple said.

"Birds of a feather?"

"Right. We had a drink together and then came on here for the meeting. We're both staunch supporters."

"Do you make each other blush?"

"Well, we haven't yet."

"Which reminds me," Jennifer said efficiently. "I have to get a couple of facts from Agnes. Hold the fort." She got up and moved away, her sway graceful.

When he had stopped watching Jennifer Rolph's hips, fetching in their straight skirt, Apple looked down. The red case had a catch but no lock, he saw. He also saw, flicking his eyes up, that he had no observers.

Being long of arm, Apple had no need to stoop completely out of sight, merely twist as he bent, in order to reach the nearest of the two cases. He freed and lifted the lid, chose the first notebook in the pack and lifted it out to his knee. The book, dated, was the most recent. After putting it back he brought out its colleague from the pack's other side, opened it on his knee and began to scan Blushers Anonymous' original members.

He fitted last names to some of the first ones he knew, not that they meant anything to him. The same when he found *Pendleton* to pair with *Jasper*, but he memorised the address and was interested to see the occupation given as stockbroker.

Apple rifled on. Norman Smith was a trumpet player in a night club, Sam Gallego had temporary work as a house painter and Wendy Harper was employed by Her Majesty's Government.

A shadow slapped over the notebook. Startled as a surprised thief, Apple quickly looked up and around. At an oblique angle behind him stood Lady Barre, still rocking from a halt, her arms coming up for a formidable fold. An executioner would have been moved by the set of her features.

Always do something to give another explanation for your confusion, they taught in Training Five. For example, if you were suddenly faced by the mark you had been tailing, he having pulled a clever one, you could fling your arms around him and pretend you were mistaking him for your cousin, the vicar; or fight not to produce a mighty sneeze; or ask him for directions to the nearest police station, where you want to report having had your pocket picked; or act a twisted ankle, heart attack, bursting bladder, nausea; or, in extreme cases, you could accuse the mark of following you.

Letting the notebook fall was the best alternative reason for his turmoil that Apple could come up with on the hook of the moment. While bending to pick it up he put his mind ferociously to work in order to hold his incipient blush down to a grade two.

He is in a spaceship, at the controls. Directly ahead is the sun, almost filling the porthole that is remarkably like Ethel's windshield (the scene's creator, standing mentally apart, tutted at the vapidity of his imagination). The heat is incredible, as terrifying as the danger: His brakes have just failed and the steering-wheel is jammed.

"May I ask what you are doing?"

The voice's main icicle shattered the scene. Apple, his fumbling to grasp the notebook over, successful, straightened while turning, merely pink on the jaw and wearing an expression of surprised delight.

"I thought so," he said. "It's our charming mentor herself at long last."

"Just so, Mr. Porter," Lady Barre said, face and form not melting. "And I repeat my question."

"Why am I late myself tonight? Well, I can explain. It's perfectly understandable."

"That was not what I asked, young man. I want to know why you are looking at the secret and confidential Files."

After a dazed-like glance around, as though waking from a nap, Apple seemed to notice the notebook in his hand. "Oh, *this*," he said. He gave a jolly laugh. "Yes indeed."

"Indeed what?" Lady Barre asked from over her folded arms. Her crimson bib-overall looked to be strained to its limits.

"I was having a little peek to see if my name had been spelled right. One cares about these things. It only has one T, y'know."

"Curious way to spell Porter."

"Mmm," Apple said as he stooped. After he had put the book back in the pack and closed the lid he rose, not so much out of the polite thing to do as to obtain the psychological advantage of vastly superior height. It didn't work.

Lady Barre leaned backwards in such a way as to make it appear that she was still looking down at him. She said, spacing the words like thrown stones, "If you would be kind enough to pass me those two cases, Mr. Porter."

Apple obliged like an eager lackey. Before accepting them Lady Barre unfolded her arms as deliberately as if she were taking off a pet python. "Thank you."

"Not at all, not at all," Apple beamed, feeling his blush retreating. "My pleasure."

Lady Barre moved away. She went down the hall and found a place to sit near the front. Apple also went front-ward, but on the opposite side. There were no empty places beside Wendy so he squatted at the end of her row. She looked around at him with a nod of familiarity which he found soothing and encouraging. He refused to think ahead, however. He had been through that kind of thing before.

The person presently undergoing the agony of mass attention was a tubby fortyish man. He was either brave or a masochist. As he answered questions from the floor, he stood erect, head up, arms neatly at his sides like an escapologist waiting for the chains and locks.

It all reminded Apple of that scene in the movie version of *The Thirty-nine Steps*. But he couldn't remember what profit the hero had gained by questioning the memory man on the stage. Really, Apple decided, it was not like *The Thirty-nine Steps* at all.

The tubby man left. Immediately, Lady Barre got up, making as she did a staying motion to her secretary. She strode toward the platform as though she wanted to do it an injury. Apple alerted, like an old cat that sees a lame mouse.

On the platform Lady Barre stood facing front. With none of her customary exuberance she said, "Ladies and gentlemen, good evening. As you can see, the idea of an association of fellow sufferers, those prone to excessive blushing, has proved viable. In an amazingly short time, Blushers Anonymous has grown from a handful of people to this large group, and no doubt the story is unfinished. I have been assured by several members that already they have found easement and solace in the association. It is all most gratifying."

The audience murmured and somebody said, "Hear hear."

Lady Barre gave a meaningless smile, the type used by a hostess when red wine gets spilled on the damask. Several members, obviously assuming her little speech to be over, applauded.

When that had pattered away Lady Barre said, "The rest is up to you, ladies and gentlemen. The time has come for me to bow out of the picture."

Apple exchanged a raised-eyebrows look with Wendy. Next, he used his tallness to crane a look at Jennifer Rolph. She wore an expression of puzzlement as well as one of those just-in-case smiles.

Lady Barre was saying that her decision came at this time partly on account of other, pressing commitments, partly because of her migraine headaches, partly because soon Meen Hall would be entering a reconstruction programme and wouldn't be available for months.

"But another venue could easily be found, of course," Lady Barre went on, slapping at a stray hank of hair as though to show that she wasn't completely out of character here. "I dare say you will elect from among yourselves an organizing committee. You must try not to allow your sensitivity to stop you from being firm and constructive. As I said, it's up to you. The future of Blushers Anonymous, ladies and gentlemen, is in your hands." She bowed. "Good night and farewell."

The rest was confusion. Like gossip time in a convent, everybody talked at once. Large and small groups formed. Two men in different locations clapped their hands for attention, apparently stricken with dreams of leadership. A dozen people surrounded Lady Barre and Jennifer Rolph as they moved at a people-caused shuffle toward the exit passage. Several members looked genteelly furious.

Apple and Wendy stood together to watch. Everyone was standing. The noise bounced back down from the ceiling like falling waterbeds.

As more people crowded around, the progress of Jennifer and Lady Barre ground to a crawl. The shrug exchanged by Apple and Wendy stated that yes, there was no sense in trying to talk, battle the noise. It could wait.

When the confusion and racket became squeezed to ferocious by people going into the passage, where the caretaker and members of the next group were trying to come in the opposite direction, Apple turned toward the rear.

He said, "There has to be an emergency exit."

Wendy said, "Let's see."

Through a door behind the platform they came to a standard push-bar exit which took them into a service lane. As they walked along in the darkness Wendy took Apple's arm.

He asked, "Worried about rag-makers?" Neither of them, he recognised, was ready yet to talk about what had just happened in respect of Blushers Anonymous.

"Worried? No, not when I'm with big you."

"That's the nicest thing anyone's said to me in ages."

"And I could only say it because it's dark," Wendy said. "I'll curtsy, if you like."

"Never mind," Apple said. "Hungry?"

"Starving."

"I move that we go and put ourselves on the outside of some food."

"Seconded."

"Race you to Ethel."

Apple let Wendy win, for which he but mildly despised himself. He recovered fast by allowing her to open the driver's door for him. She got in behind and they drove off.

So as to keep his mind from counting chickens regarding Wendy's overnight accommodation, and saving Lady Barre's unexpected action for later, Apple pondered the kidnapping that they were being so casual about.

Accepting that most of the story was true, as he did, and that it had not been part of a rag, what could have been the point? The most likely answer was that the enemy had intended to get what information they could out of their prisoner, by fairly foul means or fouler. Also likely was that they had merely wanted to throw a scare into Wendy—hence that too-easy escape. But what were they scaring her about, or away from?

There were other questions. Apple sifted through them without finding any answers. The sole conclusion he reached was that the kidnap victim must know more than she was willing to tell.

The cafeteria was noted far and wide for its stew, said the girl who was ladle-poised avid to serve it. Meekly, Apple acquiesced. Coolly, Wendy chose boiled cod, which, Apple mused defensively as they carried their trays to a table, looked gaunt.

The subject of greatest moment stayed unbroached until they were fiddling with their peaches and cream. Wendy asked, "So what's it all about, Appleton?"

"Well," he said, "let's first consider the possibilities."

"Wait a minute. I think we should first consider if Lady B was telling the truth."

"Why shouldn't she be?"

"I have no idea," Wendy said. "Except it looked to me as if she was disgruntled about it all."

"I got the same impression, I'll admit."

"Of course, she could have been vaguely ashamed of herself for leaving. So she makes a big deal out of other commitments and migraine and the hall. She wants out, though in the nicest possible way."

Apple nodded. "She could've discovered another, better, more glamorous interest. Let's face it, the BA members are mostly wallflowers. Present company excepted, naturally."

"Naturally," Wendy said. "And yes, that could be it. Or there's no other interest but she's just not found Blushers Anonymous particularly stimulating."

"Maybe she couldn't be bothered to go through the rigmarole of finding new premises for the meetings. It isn't going to be all that easy."

"And talking of premises, is someone going to do the whole bit, organize a committee and everything?"

"I'm not, I can tell you," Apple said, pointing his spoon at himself.

"Doubt if I am either. It's not my style."

"Could be that everybody'll feel the same. Could be that this is the end of Blushers Anonymous."

Nodding, Wendy pushed her empty dish away. She said, "I can't think of any other reasons for Lady B quitting, can you?"

"No. But I do think there might have been something a slice peculiar about the whole scheme."

While yawning, Wendy said, "Oh?"

"You must be exhausted."

"That's the word. It's mostly nerves. My God, do you realise I was *abducted?*"

"I know," Apple said with a forward sway of sympathy. He added nonchalantly, "If you don't want to go back to your place tonight, you can come to mine."

Wendy looked at him squarely and openly. "You have a couch?"

"And a spare bedroom."

"Personally I like couches."

He smiled with, "It sounds as if you don't trust me."

Through another yawn: "Oh no."

Telling himself how much he appreciated her independence, to mention nothing of her reserve, Apple said, "My living room couch is nice and comfortable, except for that broken spring in the middle."

Wendy nodded absently as she got up. She asked, "Tell me, what did you mean when you said there might be something peculiar about the BA scheme?"

Apple's vague answers to the question he was still putting in different forms, and still not gaining anything from the questioner, when they got back to Ethel.

Driving, with Wendy sprawled on the back seat, whistling to keep herself from falling asleep, Apple agreed with himself that it would look too suspicious if he continued harping on the topic; this while knowing that

BA-as-plot had, for the moment, taken second place to the boy-makes-girl possibilities.

Ethel garaged, they hurried to Harlequin Mansions and up to the apartment, where Wendy insisted she wasn't too tired for the guided tour. She pronounced approval.

In the living room, Apple, chin in hand, lips pursed, stared at his couch with the doubt of a fakir looking at a feather bed. Wendy sat on it and gave fulsome bounces. She said, "This will do beautifully."

While she was in the bathroom showering Apple brought bedding from his spare room. Smiling, he assured himself that one day very soon they would have a good laugh about this sleeping arrangement.

Bed made, Apple went to the corner telephone. He dialled Upstairs. To the familiar male voice, numbers quoted, he said, "I want information, please."

"Expert information, of course."

After complimenting the man on his stinging wit, Apple gave him Jasper's full name and address. "Anything known about him will be appreciated, except if it's straight."

"Nobody's straight," the duty officer said.

"Oh, and one other thing. If you feel like it, please do tell God."

The man released a long, articulate grunt, as though to say, "I was only doing my job."

Disconnecting, Apple felt sure there would be no problem in his Control's direction, that it wouldn't matter if the man did tell, that Angus Watkin took an approving stance on his underling's tinkering with Blushers Anonymous.

But, Apple mused, wasn't the investigation over? Wasn't he clutching at the last straws of a hat which had just been chewed to shreds by a camel? Hadn't his suspicion of a Communist plot been rendered foolish?

Wendy came in, steaming lightly. She was wearing her host's screaming tartan robe, the hem of which she had turned up a foot or so and clipped into place with clothes-pegs.

"Ingenious," Apple said even though he knew very well he should be telling her how devastatingly attractive she looked with her wet hair and stark naked feet.

"Thank you," Wendy said. She flapped her arms to turn in a circle. "I hoped you wouldn't mind if I borrowed it."

Blowing out his cheeks Apple made fat gestures of munificence, as though offering his intestines, at the same time knowing he ought to be over there taking her into his arms.

"Thank you for making me feel welcome, Appleton."

"Mi casa es tu casa," he said, using the Spanish phrase because he knew of no other in any of his languages that expressed so well the ultimate in hostmanship: My house is your house.

"I don't know what that means," Wendy said, "but it has a friendly ring."

"Good," Apple said, wishing he dare give the phrase a romantic translation.

"Which reminds me, you're the foreign-language man, right?"

He nodded. In Finnish he told her that the couch did not have a broken spring.

"I hope that's respectable."

In English: "I'm afraid it is."

Laughing, Wendy said, "That's what surprised me tonight in the hall, when I looked back and saw Lady Barre glaring at you. Appleton's far too respectable to have said something offensive, I thought."

Hiding his wash of despair, Apple told her about the business of the red cases. "It was nothing."

"Aren't you the nosy one, though. Were you looking for my particulars?"

"Not especially."

"I'll tell you, if you like."

"Only if you want to."

Wendy lurched into a yawn. When she had shattered it off she said, "I'm falling asleep."

Apple said, "Er—listen."

She sat on the couch. "Yes?"

"Do you—um—have any ideas as to who that woman might be? The one in your room."

"No," Wendy said. She looked at him squarely again. "I'm slow at putting two and two together."

"Okay then, I'll let you get to sleep."

"Thank you."   ·

"Good night, Wendy."

"Good night, Appleton."

They each said good night three times and sleep well twice before Apple left the room and closed the door.

After finishing in the bathroom, and after putting on his secret, hidden bolt that prevented the main door from being opened from either side, Apple took himself off to bed.

Having given his pillow a thorough, grumpy punching, he settled down under the covers to have a think about Lady Barre's curious abdication.

First he saw from the angle of her being herself responsible for, or part of, a plot. She could have quit because Blushers Anonymous was getting too big, therefore unmanageable for one person, as well as more public. Or because there was the threat of a takeover from other enemy sources with the power and personnel that she lacked. Or because she had found already the perfect victim, maybe victims, and couldn't handle any more, in addition to being quite satisfied. Or because she suspected one of the members of being on to her game, investigating; which member could be Appleton Porter.

If Lady Barre was innocent, Apple thought on, an unwilling pawn in the scheme, she could have retired on account of the plotters now wanting her out, for any number of reasons: fear that she might blow it with her eccentric ways, the fact that she was proving to be a liability, the risk of her starting to smell a rodent.

That last, Apple liked. Maybe Lady Barre had just discovered the existence of a plot, he offered, and was getting out without saying anything, either to her manipulators or anyone else, since exposure of what she knew would put her in danger. She could be in danger anyway, simply by reason of being no longer of any use to the plotters.

So perhaps the answer lay not with Lady Barre but in who now took over the leadership, Apple mused without enthusiasm. And perhaps there was no answer other than Lady Barre had quit out of boredom and no plot existed.

Frustrated in more ways than one, Apple sat up to give his pillow another good punching.

The doorbell brought him up from sleep, out of his dream. In it he had been lounging on a throne, attended by two gorgeous women. One had short hair, the other green eyes. Both, dressed in the purest white, were vying for his attention, with which he was being stingy.

Apple shoved up to an elbow. His watch said it was nine o'clock—late for him and due to a restless night. Lying down again, snuggling, cozy, he ordered himself not to feel guilty about letting the doorbell go unanswered, as the neighbour who wanted to borrow a cup of sugar or ask the right time or whatever could easily go to another door.

Apple lay taut, body steeled to resist the next ring, mind trying to think of something else. His undercurrent hope was that he would get back to that dream.

When another ring didn't come Apple relaxed and got out of bed. Human nature, he knew, would not allow a person to give a single ring, not if the aim was to summon an occupant.

Trenchcoat on in lieu of robe, Apple went along the hall. An envelope had been slid under the main door. He picked it up, tore it open and drew out a folded document. It, he saw, was Ethel's new log-book; new, that is, in manufacture; ageing processes had created a worn affair complete with beer-glass rings, fluffy corners and scribbled sums.

There was no accompanying note, nothing written on the Woolworth envelope. Apple knew that were he to go mad and tell the world that, through his British Intelligence connexions, he had been able to acquire, for personal use, a false log-book, this would be denied boredly by Upstairs.

Unable to wait, understanding now that absurdity of entering a son for Eton as soon as possible after his birth, Apple went to the living room to telephone. He stopped in the door frame and almost raised a finger to his lips.

Wendy was asleep under the covers, unseen except for one arm that dangled to the carpet. She gave out a faint, musical snore, like three blind-drunk mice trying to harmonise. Apple didn't have the heart to risk waking her.

Withdrawing, door softly closed, he went to his bedroom for coins and slippers. Back at the main door he took off his secret lock and went out.

As he had hoped, once Apple got down in the street he felt a thoroughgoing profligate for wearing only slippers and being naked under his trenchcoat. He watched people to see if they noticed his feet, thought, If they only knew the rest of it, and told himself that all this was to keep his mind from fretting if Wendy would be safe while he was gone.

In the telephone kiosk of the corner newspaper shop, Apple dialled a number. Stanley Field answered promptly in his bicycle-repair shed, dismissed the earliness-apology by saying he had been up since six, as always, said, "Didn't expect to hear from you again."

"I've been extremely busy," Apple said, airy as a cloud. "But now I have some free time. Could I present my vehicle for inspection within the next few days?"

"Well as to that, the executive committee of the Antique London Taxicab Owners Guild is meeting this morning at eleven, as it happens."

"That's handy."

"Or there'll be another meeting a week from now."

"I'll be busy again by then," Apple said, hoping he was giving the impression that he was doing ALTOG a favour.

"We wouldn't normally run a test at such short notice, but I think we can make an exception, particularly as you've touted your ve-hicle so highly."

"Not without good reason."

"That," Stanley Field said with grated relish, "remains to be seen."

When Apple disconnected, address in head, he left the shop and went jauntily home. After checking on Wendy, he hummed through a shower and dressing, breakfast and the writing of an explanatory note. The last he took creepingly into the living room and propped where it could be seen.

Apple left his apartment, set off for the garage. So as not to worry about Wendy being safe, despite knowing that she would be anyway, he worried about the document which he had put carefully in his pocket.

The log-book was illegal and therefore a social crime, Apple agreed, but he defended that, to begin with, it was for Ethel more than for himself. Next, the crime had to be accepted as part of an inoperable modern growth, the OK-ness of closet corruption. Did the leaders of nations always tell the truth? Did newspapers give unbiased reports? Were judges always fair and impartial?

But you needn't consider the abstract, Apple mused. There was physical evidence on every side, the abuses that everyone took for granted, accepted, ignoring that yesteryear these factors would have been immoral or criminal: advertising dishonesty, foodstuffs only two-thirds the size of their packets, built-in obsolescence, meatless meat products. Even as recently as TV's youth, canned laughter would have been considered an abuse.

The gradual decay had begun, Apple acknowledged, when the spinning jenny formed an illicit relationship with the steam engine, producing a bastard called the Industrial Revolution. The world could no more start dismantling its falsities than it could return to the bucolic days before that bloodless coup. The lie was not only here to stay, it was growing more bare-faced.

Whistling loudly, feeling a pleasant gripe of sleaziness and sophistication, Apple arrived in the gloom of the underground garage. He declined to recognise that if the world could go back it would also be regressing to the corruptions of disease, child labour and a hundred other ills, now largely deceased.

Apple stopped beside Ethel. She was reasonably clean, as per customary, but that wasn't good enough. Additionally there were dozens of details to be seen to, the minutiae that ALTOG's executive committee were sure to seek out with the cruel diligence of mothers looking for dirt in ears.

Apple set to work. He washed and wiped, fiddled and scraped in an ablution/titivation that was not the thorough painstaking day-long deal he had originally envisioned.

By ten-thirty he had to finish. He felt he had done as well as could be expected within the time limit. Although he knew he ought to have waited until next week, he distantly recognised that he needed all this fret and fuss to take his mind from Blushers Anonymous.

The same applied to his stimulation as he drove, as well as to his panic every time another car veered close or a double-decker came rearing up behind. He sat at the wheel caught between fun and fear. By the time he arrived he was as jittery as a bridegroom who shouldn't have had that final one at the stag party.

It was one of those suburban pubs that stand in the middle of ample concreted parking; pubs built in Thirties Ancient, with leaded windows and half timbering and lurching eaves.

Apple parked and went in. On entering the lounge bar he saw the group from ALTOG at once, Stanley Field being prominent among the six men who stood at the bar's end. He came forward, twitching inside a Sunday-best as though it were a hair shirt. After shaking Apple's hand gravely he drew him across to meet the others.

They were aged between forty and seventy, dressed from cheap-neat to foppish. Their various occupations, Apple learned in whispers from Stanley Field when, introductions over, the committee set about examining the log-book, included plumbing, dentistry and ownership of three newspapers.

The publisher, Lord March, said with a taste of doubt, "It's in remarkably good condition."

The plumber said with lifted lip. "Bit battered, if anyone was to ask me, like."

His lordship, deferentially: "Actually, you're quite right, Mr. Smith. It is rather on the battered side."

"Downright bleedin' tatty, in fact."

"Quite so, Mr. Smith. Tatty indeed."

Lord March's taxi was a 1931, Apple learned from a Stanley Field aside, whereas Jim Smith owned a 1927.

Another man said, "Good sign when they're showing a bit of age." He finished scrutinising the document through a Holmesian magnifying glass and passed it on.

It finished with the dentist, whose examination was brief. He said, "All those who accept the documentation as genuine and untampered with, say Aye."

"Aye," everyone said, including Apple by way of encouragement. The others ignored him.

Handing the log-book back the dentist said, "Now for the vehicle in question, gentlemen. The inspection. Do we have all our equipment? Good. Then let us adjourn outdoors."

Unafraid of that magnifying glass and the mysterious cases carried by some of the men, Apple proudly led the way. Outside, drummed by the pounding of many feet on concrete, he strode toward where Ethel stood ready and gleaming.

The reason Apple slowed and then stopped was because the drumming from behind had ended. He turned.

Four of the men were staring past him, one was looking at the ground as if in confusion, Stanley Field was walking back into the pub with back rigid.

Apple asked, "Yes?"

Following another bout of silent staring, Lord March and another man also turned away, faces dead, Jim Smith muttered something about a bleeding sacrilege and the dentist showed his crooked teeth to say a curt, "Inadmissible."

Apple: "What's that?"

"The rules of ALTOG make plain, sir, that the vehicle's state must be as close to the original as possible. That, of course, includes paintwork. Good day to you, sir." He and the remaining others turned away.

Apple was stunned. Ethel, he tried to digest, had been rejected. She had been summarily turned down because she wasn't painted that dreary standard black. It was an injustice, gross and shocking.

Just who the Biblical-sense did these people think they were?—Apple fumed, his face twitching. They were guilty of outright intolerance, disgusting colour prejudice, slander.

Resisting the clarion call to go marching in there and give the nose-drips a piece of his mind, Apple got back into Ethel. He was in a daze of ire and shock.

The daze lasted during the slack drive to Bloomsbury, where automatically he steered into the dim garage and over to the slot marked *Porter.* He got out.

The one positive aspect of his daze was that afterwards Apple was able to use it to explain why he stood there without acting, until it was too late to act, when the ether-soaked blanket was thrown over his head.

Beginning to come out of it he thought, I am lying on a soiled mattress in an opium den. I was forced to sample wares while following a trail through some of the lowest dives in London. I have been hitting bottom.

Despite these thoughts Apple was quite prepared to find himself in his own bed, with a cold, nasal spray at hand. It came as a shock when, conscious, he realised he was in a soaring helicopter.

His hands were tied behind, his legs were bound together below the knees, he was strapped into the seat, he wore a gag. Although the blanket had gone, there was an efficient blindfold over his eyes.

The noise and movement were as deafening and as turbulent as driving a tractor with a busted silencer cross-wise over a ploughed field. From the first, Apple knew the aircraft to be no longer in its youth, the other told him they were flying at a considerable height.

He didn't mind the ear-smiting racket, was unperturbed by the way he was being rumpled about, could stand the pitch darkness and the chill wind that constantly blew. He felt fine. He knew that finally the caper had broken open.

The flight continued.

Unable to tell, sense, how closely he was being kept under observation, if at all, Apple confined himself to trying to judge his bonds.

He wanted to know of his rope manacle not only if it was Houdiniable but also if it had been applied by an expert. In respect of his blindfold, he easily came to the conclusion, from its efficiency, difficult to accomplish, that it wasn't the work of an amateur, unless a lucky one.

Of one thing Apple was fairly certain: he was not going to finish up in a Maida Vale kitchen; though that was all he cared to venture about destination.

For no particular reason, he rocked his head against the seat. At once he was touched. One pair of hands strayed checkingly over his bonds, blindfold and gag. That meant at least two people, he reckoned, unless the helicopter was on automatic. The hands left.

Speed was impossible to gauge. As time passed, however, with no change in conditions, Apple realised they must be covering hundreds of miles, even discounting the flying that had been done during the unknown length of time when he had been unconscious.

After roughly an hour, by Apple's count, which he found easier to make than forming an opinion about his rope manacle, all turbulence abruptly stopped. Next, the noise began on a progressive reduction. They were going down.

The landing was gentle. After the motor had died and with it the wind, Apple felt the pair of hands get to work. They released him from the seat-belt and jerked him to his feet, pulled him this way and that way and down, pushed him into an awkward hop-shuffle.

The surface underfoot was rough, the going difficult. All Apple could do in the form of protest was make gurgles through his gag. Once when he did have a try at resistance, the owner of the hands swore at him.

The voice was female. The language was German. The accent came from the Red side of the Wall.

Not only was Apple intrigued by the fact that he had been brought to East Germany, it seemed, but also by the realisation that he found the voice familiar. He resisted again in order to hear another sample. He got a kick on the ankle.

After a traipse of perhaps a hundred metres in a cold damp breeze, Apple was hustled into an interior. More hustling, and he was snapped to a halt. The hands went to the back of his head, released the gag.

Clapping his mouth like a wine-taster, Apple said, "That's better. Go on."

But that was the last touch from the hands. Next came the sound of a door closing and of a bolt being scraped home.

Cautiously, Apple shuffled in what he guessed to be the door's direction, moving sideways so as not to lead with his head. When his shoulder touched a solid, he changed position to make the same touch with his ear. It was on wood.

With one faculty cut off or restricted, the others were heightened, Apple knew. You could see better if you plugged your ears, and you could hear better if you closed your eyes. You could hear even better still if you had had your eyes closed for quite some time, such as behind a blindfold.

What Apple could hear through the door now was movement, a person being busy, or restless. He guessed himself to be in a room inside a building.

He tensed as the voice came again. It was talking to someone who didn't answer, who, obviously, was on the other end of a telephone line.

They had arrived safely and without incident, the woman said, still speaking German. The prisoner would be ready for questioning in two or three hours, when he settled from the ether and the journey. No, she didn't know whether force would be necessary or not, but she had the impression that it wouldn't be, that he would be sensible.

Lovely, Apple thought with a niggle of concern, while at the same time reminding himself triumphantly that his scientist ploy had worked and that he had been right all along about Blushers Anonymous.

The woman ended her call in commonplaces which Apple found a shade offensive, considering the situation. He went on listening. Soon he heard a door close. After that there was nothing. He had the feeling that the speaker had gone out.

First, Apple thought, let's deal with the blindfold. That chore, as he recalled from Training Three, was done not by trying to press it up, but down; down, that is, when the head itself was turned downward.

So, bending double from the waist, Apple got the back of his head against the door. He began to give deep nods in reverse, scraping his blindfold against the wood.

Nothing happened. Despite that, despite feeling stupid, he scraped diligently on. His neck started to ache and his head felt as though it were swelling and the backs of his legs were killing him. He scraped on.

It was when the most prominent of all the pains he had was the most recent, at the curve of his head, that Apple knew he was winning. The blindfold had started to move; it was dragging on his hair.

Slowly, the band of material went over the curve. It came off with a rush, dropping. Apple blinked as he glared his animosity at the circle of black cloth lying on the floor.

He began to straighten, which ended his glare because he needed to pull a face to match his whimpers.

Five minutes passed before his head had shrunk to normal and the pains in various parts of his body had faded, he meanwhile helping by waving himself languorously like a fern underwater. He also accustomed his eyes to the light and took careful stock of his surroundings.

He was in an end section of a barn-like building, he judged: three walls were of brick, the dividing wall was composed of cinder-block. The roof, high, was corrugated-tin sheeting. The door was solid. Opposite it, twenty feet away on the end wall, was a window of pebbled glass, three feet long and one foot deep, covered with thick, close-set bars. Furniture comprised an empty-can toilet and a wooden-box seat.

It wasn't the most secure of cells, Apple granted gratefully, but then the enemy wouldn't be expecting their prisoners to have any escape knowledge.

Apple thought about method as he started on the software manacle. Rope, as he was aware, had its strength built in longwise, not across, therefore he didn't waste any time on trying to force his wrists apart. He set about pushing one hand down, the other up.

There was progress. Presently the fingers of his right hand were in the palm of the left. He was aided by the rope being not cold, which made hemp tight, but warm, which rendered it loosely soft. This was because the manacle had been pressed between his body and the helicopter seat.

While wriggling his wrists Apple went on pushing and lifting, the pressure on the rope thus being oblique. The backs of his wrists grew sore but the more they were gouged into by the rope the more space there would be for extrication.

Apple froze. He fancied he had heard a noise from outside. Closing his eyes to listen he wondered if he should try a butting attack if anyone came in. But, he realised, even if he got out he wouldn't travel very far with rear-tied arms and hobbled legs.

There were no more noises. Nerves, Apple told himself as he opened his eyes and went back to work. He reversed hands, sending the right down and pulling on the left. His fingers climbed steadily, the pain of gouging made him grimace like an untipped cabbie and the possibility of his wrists bleeding made him glare a don't-you-dare, for liquid would cause the hemp to tighten.

As his fingers climbed, so did the rope descend, scrape steadily and painfully over the back of his left hand. In another minute he was free.

Rope flung aside, Apple rubbed his wrists gently but didn't look at them in case it made him feel queasy. He did look at the manacle, noting that it had a professional neatness.

Following another listen with his ear on the door Apple bent over to the next job, and listened again once the rope had been removed from around his legs.

Now came the final problem—escape from confinement. Which, Apple had concluded, had to be made through the roof. Both door and window were breachable but needed time, and time was of the essence, said essence being composed of the attar of fear.

Although Apple realised that he may have been meant to overhear the telephone conversation, that wasn't to say the enemy had no intentions of playing rough to gain cooperation. And he couldn't cooperate because he wasn't really a scientist, which they weren't likely to believe, and play would get rougher. He didn't want to know about that.

In the name of silence Apple refrained from taking the wooden box apart with well-aimed kicks, even though he would have enjoyed doing so, perhaps while dwelling on ALTOG's executive committee. To lever the box into the needed separate slats he used his penknife, which then came in handy for pressing out one of the two nails from each end of every slat. It also, wrapped in a handkerchief for muffling, served well as a hammer.

Nailing the slats across a rear corner of the room was the simplest chore yet. Why builders didn't use cement between bricks Apple had no idea, such information being too practical to fire his interest, but he was grateful for what they did use, mortar, which offered feeble resistance.

When each slat, each step in his ladder, had been fixed in place by means of its already-present nail, Apple secured it with another. He worked quietly, steadily.

After he had double-nailed slats to as far up as he could reach, which was not an inconsiderable height, he continued his work by standing on the first step, delicately, and remembering to set his feet at the ends.

He went on in this manner until he ascended to within close touch of his goal, some six metres above the

ground. The tin sheeting, when tested, had give. Tin
sheeting always did have, being the cheapest form of
roofing—and, as Apple was aware, the most difficult type
to anchor: only nails would do the job, and that with less
than perfection.

After going carefully down and up again for the last
time, to get one of the remaining slats, its nails stepped
flat, Apple started to use it as a lever on the nearest sheet.
It was already loose. Its corner came up with a whine of
acquiescence. The next connexion point was even easier.
Soon he had enough space to crawl through.

With Apple hanging from his fingertips, the drop was a
mere three metres. He pushed off as he let go, so that
when his feet hit dirt he went over backwards, lessening
the fall's shock. Also he twisted as he went. He finished in
a semi-sideways roll, from which he gained his feet in a
way that he had never been able to bring off in the gym.

On account of that and for everything else pertaining
to his escape Apple felt exceedingly clever. There was an
element of swagger in the swing of his shoulders as he set
off running over the grass.

All around were fields with hedgerow divisions—as far
as could be seen: due to a light mist, visibility stood at
some one hundred metres.

When in a moment Apple stopped to look back, after
several preliminary glances, it was because the mist was
being intensified by distance around the place he had
left, which meant he himself had become less visible
than before from there.

The place was a farm, a collection of brick buildings
with tin roofs, largest the barn he had been held in. They
had an air of semi-desertion, with no signs of livestock
and few of the oddments which were usually found lying
around farms. Apple learned nothing.

He turned and ran on, charged with the exhilaration of regained liberty. His plans were super short-term—escape from captors who might get violent. Of the long-term Apple had formed not even the sketch of a plan. He had no notion of what he was going to do in a country that was not on the friendliest of terms with his own. He didn't know what he could say if he was picked up by the police. A story of being a tourist with passport lost or stolen would last only until a check was made with Intourist, by which time he may have been located by his abductors, who, outranking the police, would happily make him their prisoner again.

Apple came to a low hedge. Jumping it in style he raced on. He felt light in spirits as well as in ego, the clever pro. Helping was the attractive mist.

It faded and thickened patchily as Apple ran, covering field after field, all lying fallow. Some hedges he jumped, the taller ones he followed until he found a gate, after climbing which he went along to roughly the non-jump point and continued from there: he wanted to keep as much as possible in a straight line, since he could see no sense in wandering.

When, presently, Apple did change course, it was because of a noise. The humming came from his oblique right and, despite his wanting to avoid civilization, he could no more resist the call than a person can disbelieve a compliment.

As the hum grew louder through proximity it became recognisable as the sound of traffic. Its constancy told that the road which lay ahead had to be a major artery.

After jumping another hedge Apple saw that he was in a final field, there being no hedgerow at the far end, merely a dropping away of the ground. The hum had turned into a collection of individual roars and rattles and rasps.

Apple reduced to a walk as he neared the field's open border. At an even slower pace he edged up to the drop. He had sunk to a squat before he came into sight of a highway.

Six lanes wide, it lay well below him down a sloping bank. Bursting from and disappearing into the mist, vehicles were speeding in both directions.

Some aspect of the traffic there was that struck Apple as peculiar. He didn't know what it was. Certainly, the private cars and commercial vehicles and motor-cycles seemed normal enough, he thought.

Shrugging, Apple rose to move on along the bank top, get within reading distance of what looked to be a signpost just inside the mist's frill down there on the roadside. Knowing what part of the country he was in would be a useful start to whatever he planned on doing.

The signpost's lettering eased clear of white vapour two seconds after Apple had realised what was wrong with the traffic: it ought to have been moving on the Continental European right, not the United Kingdom left. The signpost informed that it was eight miles to London.

Apple stopped walking. He was rendered so insecure through surprise and annoyance that he scratched his ribs like an ape. The former emotion drifting off, he was left with the growing latter. He had been completely fooled by the trick of being taken on a long, circling helicopter ride and then having German spoken at him, the accent from eastward.

Quickly Apple told himself the idea was outstandingly smart. Brilliant. Anyone at all would have been taken in by it. These people knew what they were doing, all right. Their prisoners think they've been flown to another country, where they'll have no friends and no consular protection; they're left alone in blindfolded darkness for hours after hints that if they don't cooperate they'll be dealt with harshly. Cooperation was almost guaranteed.

Apple saw that he had turned and was walking back along the bank, and, now, that he was peeling off to head retracingly across the field.

He had decided, Apple gathered, that what he had to do now was return to the farm (if he could find it) and get back into his cell-room before his absence was discovered (if he could manage that). Both could prove difficult if not impossible. Replacing his bonds would be simple.

The idea, Apple pointed out to himself because he didn't feel particularly enamoured of his intention, was to see what happened next, or to find out what these people wanted, or to get a look at them by throwing off the manacle and pushing up the blindfold, or to effect a capture.

In answer Apple offered that what would happen next was sure to be messy, that what these people wanted was what he, the phony scientist, could not give, that there were easier/safer ways of getting a look at the enemy, and that effecting a capture sounded fine so long as it didn't involve half a dozen armed spooks.

Apple decided not to make any decisions until he got there because arrival might not happen, due to getting lost, although, shrewdly, he had taken as near a straight line away as he could, therefore the retracing of steps right back there shouldn't be all that difficult.

Away from the highway's bank Apple started to jog. Spurred by the thought of how courageous he was being, he went in the sprightly manner of a truant.

To avoid dwelling on the reality of what he was feeling courageous about, Apple admitted to having a tinge of disappointment. He had been secretly looking forward to escaping to the West, hiding out, travelling by night, stealing food and clothing, doing all manner of tough-isms and depredations in the perfectly understandable name of self-preservation. He gave a poignant smile.

With directions Apple had no trouble. He jumped hedges in the same places, climbed the same gates, crossed the same fields. Long before expected, the farm buildings came peeking through the mist as prettily as a village in dreamland.

Apple slowed to a halt, noting that nothing had changed ahead. After a pause to let his breathing get back to normal and to remind himself about that courage, he went forward at a tense walk.

From the buildings came silence. No hen clucked, no dog growled, no bird whistled. Like a sick bandit, it was depressing more than menacing.

Apple saw that unless there was a ladder around, getting back into his cell would be an impossibility. Cheered, but nervous of what rashness he might get up to, he reached the corner of the barn where he had landed from his drop.

He began to creep along the side. There was still nothing to be heard. He came to a door. Carefully trying the handle he found it unlocked. With caution but emboldened by that corpse silence he eased the door open.

The first thing he saw was another door, in the cinderblock wall to his left, the wall of his cell. The door stood open wide. Nodding to himself that his escape had been discovered, he went inside and looked at the rest of the barn.

It was mostly bare. There was little to see other than a cluster of machinery on the far side, near where huge double-doors stood open in the end wall.

Apple walked that way. When he was alongside the machinery he slapped to a stop, pulled up short by realisation. He had found his helicopter.

The old tractor with a busted silencer couldn't be improved on as a creator of noise and vibrations, the junked armchair perched atop planking on the rear wheels served perfectly as a chopper seat, the ordinary domestic fan on the radiator not only supplied the wind but also drove tell-tale exhaust fumes toward the open doubledoors.

Masterful, Apple allowed with a hand-waggle of respect. After gazing his fill he turned in a circle, seeing how he had been walked out through the big doors, around the barn side, in again and into the end-section cell.

Looking back at the imitation helicopter he gave another gesture of respect for a particularly neat aspect: the whole set-up could be operated by two people or even one.

And talking of people, Apple reminded himself. But he knew there was nobody at all around; knew the enemy would have taken off for parts mysterious as soon as the prisoner's absence was discovered.

Which disturbing discovery could only have been made minutes ago, Apple realised. So why didn't he start on the steps of elimination? First off, why didn't he telephone Lady Barre to see if she was there?

The glances which Apple darted eagerly around soon showed him that the barn had no telephone. That overheard conversation involving one person, therefore, had after all been part of the psychological build-up. Again, Apple shook respect off a hand.

Next, he nodded. This was in agreement with himself that he had to get to a telephone as soon as immediately. He raced out through the big doors.

Unfortunately for his sense of drama, Apple had to stop racing almost at once. He accepted that it would be stupid to leave here without checking to make sure that there was, as per his conviction, no one around.

Mouth sour, he checked, looking via windows in all the other buildings, briefly and with more exasperation than prudence. There was no one around. Turning from the last window he flapped his arms heavily against his sides, miming, *See?*

Apple ran along a dirt lane away from the farm. Ahead lay only mist, a woozy curtain hiding mystery. That he hadn't headed for the known, the highway, was because hitching a ride, he felt sure, would involve a lengthy wait.

He knew, however, that since open country was in limited supply this close to London's rim, there had to be life close at hand. One small cottage would do, so long as it was equipped with a telephone.

Apple grinned: through the mist a fence had appeared. Next came a five-barred gate, open right back and giving onto a road that was narrow but with a hard-top surface. The gate had a name-plate: Pewter Farm.

Apple's grin congealed slightly when, having passed through onto the road, he was smitten by anxiety. Some atavistic order, social urge or fatuous sentiment forced him to swing back. He closed the gate.

Running on, Apple let his grin's tacky remains fade away. Not that he allowed his face to grow solemn, for by some supernatural means in which he didn't believe for a moment this could encourage dwellings to remain elusive.

On either side of the road were scruffy hedges and stretches of age-rotted fencing. That, along with the silence beyond the batter of Apple's footfalls, gave an impression of somewhere far from civilization.

To ignore the suggestion that he could be heading even further into the wilds, Apple dwelled again on the smoothness of the enemy's kidnap scheme. When the prisoner had, hopefully, been drained of information, the ether-chopper routine would be reversed and he would come round to find himself in a field somewhere (anywhere far from here, taken hence by car). He would believe he had been returned to Britain from abroad. Thankful for that, ashamed of having talked, he most likely would never mention the episode to a soul.

A scheme all-round smooth and neat, Apple acknowledged. And it would have worked like a lucky charm if he hadn't cleverly broken it open.

Feeling on top again Apple ran harder. He was not lacking in appreciation of the scene—the deserted countryside, the romantic near-fog, the secret agent racing against time to a date with destiny. He kept his smile inside.

On hearing a car coming along from behind, Apple didn't stop but semi-turned and held out a thumb-sprout hand. The car swept past without slowing. Despite knowing that under the circumstances he would have done exactly the same, Apple sneered. It made him feel hard as well as clever.

His smile did come out as a darkness in the mist ahead took shape. It turned into a house. Another house appeared opposite and then there were others, a line on either hand. Apple ran on. Other cars went by and he enjoyed ignoring them.

The road widened, the buildings became small businesses. They were all closed for lunch. Apple continued running until he saw the expected, a telephone booth. It was outside a post office, closed also but with small ads in a glass case on the wall. Several of the advertisements were of radio taxis and Apple had memorised one of the blare-printed telephone numbers before he reached the booth.

Inside, door propped, he dialled that number first in spite of his urgency to call Viceroy House. Only a couple of minutes would be taken up and he might have even greater need of transportation than he had now.

A man with a lazy voice answered. Apple, glancing at the district's name on the post office, said, "Taxi, please. I'm calling from the Hammerstowe box."

"Oh, all right," the man said, like someone agreeing to get out of bed, in a while, if he didn't fall asleep again. "Be there in fifteen minutes."

"Can't you make it any faster?"

"There's never any real hurry, in my experience."

"In this case there is."

The man asked a slow, "What?"

Apple juggled between a plane to catch, a wife about to give birth (he could make it twins), a bride waiting at the church and a luncheon date at 10 Downing Street, absorbing duringly that the man sounded young, early twenties.

Apple heard himself say, "Roland Rocque."

Laziness gone: "Did you say Roland Rocque?"

"I did."

"That's you?"

"No," Apple said. "I take care of his sequins."

"No kidding."

"I have to get some new ones to him soonest. He's flipping. You know how it is with drummers."

Sounding as if he wished he did: "Right."

"So there's a bit of a panic on."

"Be there in three and a half minutes," the man said, beating the words out rapidly like bongo thunks before disconnecting.

Eyes sardonically narrow, Apple dipped the cradle with a blasé finger. These trifling matters, he told himself, were easily dealt with if a man knew what was what in the modern world.

The next call was to Viceroy House. A receptionist, male, answered crisply. When Apple asked to be connected with the Barre suite, he said, "Lady Barre has left instructions that she is not to be disturbed."

His voice raised, Apple said, "This is Lady Barre's personal physician speaking, Sir Philip Pewter."

"I have my orders, Sir Philip."

"Perhaps she's gone out."

"No, Lady Barre checks out at two o'clock. Two sharp. The car has been ordered."

Apple tried a cunning "Destination?"

"I have no idea," the receptionist said, crisper. "Good day." The line clicked off.

Putting down the receiver, Apple thought about it. The matter of Lady Barre's whereabouts remained unanswered, but she would be findable at two o'clock, and followable, perhaps to somewhere or someone of great interest. It was the only possible move.

Apple looked at his watch. It told him flatly that he had less than an hour until two. It would be just about enough time, he figured—*if* he could get to Ethel fast enough. Ethel had to be used, as it was too late to go through the rigmarole of renting a car, and trying to tail someone secretly in a taxi was out of the question.

Apple's third and final call was to Upstairs. The man who answered had a familiar sigh in his voice. He said, "It's you."

"Yes."

"We're on an information kick at the moment, if memory serves me right."

"It does," Apple said. "You've got something for me?"

The duty officer sounded happy to announce, "No."

"Never mind. Here's a new request. I want a check

made on a farm out Hammerstowe way to see who
rented it recently or has permission to use it or whatever."

While Apple was speaking a radio-cab came to a
screeching stop alongside the telephone booth. The stan-
dard-model car's driver, who had a shaven head and a
black leather T-shirt, stared into the booth expectantly,
proudly and perkily. He gave eager little nods.

Apple made him the thumbs-up sign while giving the
duty officer what details he had on Pewter Farm. He felt
busy and accomplished and productive, as well as clever
and hard, a man of many facets.

"I think I ought to mention that this is an Urgent
Two," he said into the receiver.

"You're out of touch," the duty officer said like a hum.
"Nowadays we have an Urgent Three."

"I know," Apple lied. "I know."

"How about if I put you down for that?"

Ignoring the possibility of a put-down implication, not
wanting to get paranoid, Apple said coolly, "A Two will
do me splendidly, thank you."

"It's your funeral, to coin a phrase."

"What you can do is note that this is an LSH. I'll be in
quiet pursuit of a certain Lady Barre starting from Viceroy House at two o'clock this afternoon."

A Last Seen Heading, which Apple had never had the
opportunity of using before, and was using now mainly
for that reason, gave Upstairs a clue to work on or be
amused about in case you were never heard of again.

From outside came a series of rapid blasts on the radio-
cab horn. Apple nodded through the glass.

The duty officer asked, "Anything else?"

"Not right at this moment," Apple said. "I don't have
the time available to contact Weapons, arm myself."

"You could always try making a catapult."

Since there had been another horn-blast, a long one, while the duty officer had been speaking, Apple was able to say, "Sorry, I can't hear you." Showing a flat, restraining hand to the cabbie, who, face lively, was making forward jerks with his trunk, Apple ordered in pro, agent-in-the-field style, "Now let's have some action from you desk people up there. Over and out." He knew he would hate himself later for the squelch, but at the moment it was sweet.

Flinging out of the booth and over to the taxi, he got in behind its driver and said a terse "Let's go."

FIVE

London's fringes, the tediously nice-normal red-brick edges of a core that was interesting if void of charm, always put Apple in mind of an aluminium frame around a dirty picture. Today, they slid by painlessly in the mist.

The driver sat over his wheel in a hunch of determination, T-shirt and ears on close terms. As he was reminiscent of that morose Before man of those advertisements in which the After man looks ecstatic under a wig, Apple had privately dubbed him B4, which had a nice dossier-like ring to it.

B4 had a goal. He was being ruthless about pedestrians and insane about traffic lights as he careened toward Wood Green. That northern suburb, as glamorous as tweezers, formed the goal because Apple had asked to be taken to the nearest Underground station in his supposed dash to a West End theatre. In Greater London as in any urban sprawl, the only time a surface vehicle can compete with a subway train for dispatch is when the power fails.

Apple sat on the seat edge. He had become as tense as a sky-diver on the point of changing his mind. He could almost hear his watch ticking.

It wasn't merely that Apple was worried about the shortness of time, nor on account of having to invent acceptable answers to B4's questions about the celebrated Roland Rocque, nor that their progress had its hair-scaring aspect, but also because he was sparring with a problem.

B4 asked aside, "And who puts all them sequins back when they're ripped off by fans?"

"His mother," Apple said. "Sweet old thing. She's always there, hovering with her needle."

"Well well. To look at him you wouldn't think he had a mother."

Apple's problem was, how could he keep his tailing presence a secret in a vehicle as exotically coloured as Ethel, who was known about by Lady Barre if not actually seen? Would a car have to be rented after all? Would he finish up retaining the services of B4?

Ahead, a truck turned ponderously out of a side street, curving away in the opposite direction as it did so. It was on this side of the road, while on the other side was coming a solid line of traffic.

Though the built-up area called for a speed limit of thirty, the radio-cab was hitting seventy-five.

The next thing it would hit, Apple thought, was the truck. He tried to say, "Slow down," but the words wouldn't form, perhaps due to his having said with a scoffing laugh, when earlier B4 had asked him if he frightened easily, "Try me."

Reducing to a judicious seventy, B4, hunching more, steered into the side and bounce-jumped over the kerb. They flew along the walkway beside garden walls.

Apple closed his eyes. When he opened them again, after another bounce, the cab had returned to the road and was caught among other cars all doing the law-abider's thirty plus ten. Apple went back with relief to his problem re Ethel and the shortness of time.

B4 asked, "So listen, how does he stick the sequins on his tongue?"

"Black paint."

"You what?"

"What?"

"He sticks 'em on his tongue with black paint?"

Apple said, "Right." While he went on to explain about that material being an excellent adhesive in addition to creating a dark background for the glitter, he was telling himself that the solution to his problem was, of course, to give Ethel a coating of black, wash-off paint.

A subversive suggestion that the idea was somewhat extreme Apple managed to ignore, the way he was ignoring his suspicion that the idea had been hanging around for quite some time now, just waiting for the right opportunity to excuse its becoming noticeable.

"Christ," the driver murmured, either impressed or bemused. "Black paint yet."

"In fact I have to pick up a can of it," Apple said firmly, finalising on his idea.

"Pick up?"

"Buy. From a shop. So we'll have to stop in the next big shopping district you come to."

"Okay, but you better make it sharp."

Apple gave the deep, sweeping nod of absolute agreement. He could spare no more than five minutes for paint-buying, no more than ten for the job of painting itself—and both could be fitted into the limited time available only if this cab-ride and then the train-ride went hitchlessly.

The cab was still penned. Caught behind a line of traffic, kept from passing on the legal side by constantly approaching vehicles, on the illegal by school children, B4 surgingly ebbed and flowed, whining.

Apple would have sat even closer to the seat's edge if it weren't that his knees could go no further, being already deep into the back of the seat in front.

He had to be content with clenching the toes of one

foot and then the other, alternating rapidly, meanwhile torturing himself with lurid possibilities:

What if the radio-cab got stopped at a roadblock for that speeding and walkway bit back there? What if the hardware store had every colour but black? What if Underground staff had called a lightning strike? What if Ethel had a puncture?

As a new possibility occurred to him Apple himself whined. What if he didn't get to Viceroy House in time and some other Upstairs agent took over, stole his caper? Apple cursed his show-off idiocy in giving the duty officer an LSH.

B4 said, "Maybe he gets high on it."

"What's that?"

"The paint. Maybe it turns him on."

"Maybe it does," Apple said. Under his tension he was aware guiltily that this was how slander about the celebrated got its first big break. But he was too preoccupied to be able to mount a counter-attack.

B4 asked, "Ever try it yourself?"

Apple escaped into a near-shouted "Shops ahoy."

They were the forerunners in an extensive conglomeration, commercial core of a sprawling suburb that would have been a town if not cowed by the bully proximity of London.

The penning traffic had forced the car to slow. Apple opened the door. He began to ease his body out backwards in preparation. "Find somewhere to wait," he said. "Don't switch the motor off."

B4 snapped a grateful, "Roger."

The car stopped. Apple thrust himself out, twirled and went to the pavement. Five minutes, he warned. No chat about the weather. In, buy, out.

The paucity of pedestrians didn't strike Apple as odd until, running toward a hardware store, he saw the sign hung in its door: Closed. It was still lunchtime, he realised. Everything would be shut tight except pubs and cafes.

Apple went on to the door anyway and tried the handle, got no charity there, leaned his brow and two cupping hands on the glass. Inside sat a woman. She held sandwich and paperback. When Apple thumped with one elbow she looked around. Her face lightened. She nodded, she smiled, she turned slowly back to her food/book in a tremble of power.

Consoling himself that, if nothing else, he had made someone's day, Apple pushed off and ran on.

He turned into a side street. It was even quieter than the other, as he had expected. There was no one around when he came to a wild halt in front of a small paint shop. He noted the closed sign, the store's name, the row of wash-off products in the window and the fact that one of the cans was the colour he wanted.

What Apple didn't note as now he turned his dithering, hasty attention elsewhere, was a brick. He tutted. Even though he knew you couldn't truly expect to find bricks lying about in the streets in these tidy days, he was still scratchily irked, unable not to take it personally.

He had another, less hasty look around. Across the road stood a truck in the mid-life crisis, its low back all buckle, its front all dent. Apple ran over. On the bed, among other flotsam, lay a wheel without a tyre.

It would serve the purpose as well as anything, Apple urged himself. There was no need to look any further. And the coast was clear.

After rippingly bringing out money and separating from it a five-pound note to throw onto the bed, Apple leaned over and hoisted up and lifted out the wheel. He ran back with it. He raised it over his head as he went. He hurled it mightily ahead of him at the window.

The crash was sickening. It sounded like a head-on collision between speeding greenhouses.

The noise was still ravishing the street when Apple, thrilled by his vandalism and boldly indifferent to the fact that glass shards were falling from above, stepped into the display area. Crunching underfoot, he grabbed up a one-kilo can of black paint. He also grabbed a brush.

Leaping back outside, landing quite stylishly, he thought, Apple saw that the noise had brought the beginnings of life. In several directions people were peering long-necked as they slowly approached, bent forward from the waist and with hands raised as if to catch the reason for it all should it be thrown their way.

Darting into the middle of the roadway, Apple ran. He passed near a woman who suggested in a cautious tone, "Police?" and a man who extended a forefinger as though to say, "Now now." Then he was at the corner.

B4's car stood a hundred metres along, double-parked and with vapour popping from the exhaust-pipe. Apple raced that way. Counting in his head, he made it in eleven seconds, which he wouldn't have minded betting was a record time for someone who was handicapped by brushes and cans.

He bundled inside the radio-cab, panting. When B4 asked as he shot the car forward what that noise had been Apple said he was just about to ask the same question.

"Seemed to come from back there," B4 said.

"Sound gets echoed about," Apple offered. He took a scan behind. Only the forefinger man was watching. He had his finger on the side of his nose.

Turning, Apple sagged into the seat. Catching sight of the driver's eyes in his rear-view mirror and reading suspicion therein, he ended the matter by asking, "Are you *sure* you don't know what that noise was?"

The journey continued.

Traffic elastic, the radio-cab made good speed without having to, or being able to, perform like a deranged stock-car, which wildness Apple could stand/enjoy only if he were in charge of the driving.

Due to this safe conduct and having brought off shiningly one of his tasks, Apple semi-relaxed, at least to the extent of leaving his toes alone.

About the shop he explained to himself that it would be easy enough to ascertain the value of a window of that size (paint and brush had stick-on price tickets), and to mail a suitable cheque plus a goodly percentage extra to cover the inconvenience of being for a time windowless. The sum he would claim back from Accounts, who would scream and froth, as well as sending someone to check on the truth of the damage, before coming through with a rebate, in three or four months.

"We'll be there in a coupla minutes," B4 said. He cut in front of a bus with unnecessary rashness, the way an ex-boxer refuses to get his nose unflattened.

Apple pampered, "You've done very well."

"Wood Green's on the Piccadilly Line."

"Perfect," Apple said, in truth. There would be six or so stations to Russell Square, from where he was within an easy run of home territory.

"So listen," B4 said. "Them sequins. The bit at the end where they come shooting out of his ears. How does he do it?"

"Trade secret," Apple said. "Sorry."

Accusingly: "You told me about the black paint."

Apple leaned forward. "Actually," he said, preparing with a sluice of disappointment to shed his slander-maker guilt. "As a matter of fact." He had known all along it would come to this. "I'll be perfectly straightforward with you."

In a dead voice B4 stated, "It wasn't true."

By reliving in imagination that magnificent moment when he had hurled the wheel through the window at the same time as he was explaining to B4 about the paint story being used to hide another trade secret, Apple managed to pretend that the latter wasn't happening. It wasn't difficult. His defeatism didn't stand a chance against the act, fact and glory of destruction, which imbalance afforded Apple a comforting, compensating sensation of concern.

He arrived on the station platform out of breath. Not pounding to a halt, he graded straight into the strides of a pace-out, the while putting his ticket away so he wouldn't chew it to a grey rag.

In order not to fret about the racing seconds, or over the possibility of the police catching up at any moment, led by the forefinger man, Apple thought of B4's face as they said good-bye. Despite being deprived of inside knowledge by his fare, the driver obviously not only held no grudge but hadn't wanted his association with glamour to end. His expression at the last moment, Apple now understood, wasn't appreciation of the large tip, but envy.

Apple shivered. So seldom had he been envied in his life, could not indeed recall the last time, that it made him feel shorter by several inches.

Until he heard a train in the distance Apple strode average. He made a mental note to remind himself later to remember B4's face again.

The train came in at a chatter and gulp. Apple let the whole length go by. When the train stopped he got in its last carriage. This choice was so that every time they came into a station he could move forward one carriage by going out and getting in again, thereby giving an anodynic impression of extra progress.

The doors hissed closed, the train grumbled on its way. Unmindful of the fair collection of passengers, Apple continued his pacing. He thought it marvellous of him, mature, to take no heed of the stares, while agreeing that someday people would travel just like this in rockets to the sun.

At the next station Apple burst outside itchily. He fussed on the platform, willed boarders to look lively, got in at the ultimate second and started his pacing.

This routine he followed at every station until he ran out of carriages. On board he supplied himself with percussion by tapping brush on can and he composed letters to London Transport in complaint of the way their trains were overheated.

The front carriage, now Apple no longer wanted to pace, was all but deserted—wouldn't you know it, he thought with satisfaction. He needed to calm so that his thinking from hereon would be unflurriedly sound.

Sitting, Apple looked at his reflection in the window opposite, made mirror-like by the tunnel. Idly he lifted the brush. Its broad brown head he put on his chin to see how he would look with a beard. He had always had a secret fancy for a beard. It would grow out gingerish, of course, but a touch of dye would make it more solid.

Apple found the soft hairs pleasant against his skin. The feeling was quite sensual. While keeping the brush still he moved his head languidly from side to side, to heighten the effect closing his eyes.

Next, reversing, holding his head still, he began to stroke the brush across his mouth and jaw. It felt so good he became more thorough, put real flourish into his wrist and took in the entire face.

With the brush on its way down his nose, Apple

paused. He sensed he had an observer. Opening his eyes, looking sidelong, he saw the thin older woman who was holding one ear in consternation. He also saw, as his gaze came front, that the train was standing still and that the station was Russell Square.

The doors hissed, closing.

Apple was there fast. He got an arm through, which stopped the doors from meeting and sent them back open again. "Wait wait," he told them before dashing to the seat to get his can of paint. Back at the new-closing doors he was able to slip through, out onto the platform.

Laughing aloud to show himself how smoothly and casually he managed these things, he walked off. His mouth was dry.

The run to the garage took an estimated six and a half minutes; estimated because Apple didn't want to make himself nervous by checking the time. Never did he imagine that one kilo could become so heavy, so great a burden.

In the underground garage Apple sat on Ethel's running-board head down, regaining his breath. He was still gasping, still declining to look at his watch, when he got up to set about opening the can.

Smiling to spread good will to all things, fleshly or dumb, Apple got a screwdriver. He prised at the lid's lip. Unusually, it didn't come up alone, as soft as hot cheese; it brought with it the lid proper.

Apple would have wondered what now would go wrong to make up for that, if, he told himself, he didn't have more sense.

He started work at the back. With no time for finesse, he slapped the paint on and spread it in all directions and overlapped carelessly around the window. The lack of perfection he accepted as unimportant.

He mused that what he would do was go over the untidy bits before next Thursday when—

Apple chopped the thought off brutally. He offered not even an explanation, a retraction or an apology. He concentrated hard on his work.

When Ethel's back, one side and the front were finished, Apple allowed himself to make a check with his watch. Immediately he got nervous. Time was dangerously short. He couldn't delay another minute.

The brush he stood in the two-thirds empty can, which he put on the floor beside the driver's seat before getting in himself. Faithful Ethel started on the first buzz. Apple reversed from his slot, headed around and off and swooped up onto the street as grimly as though to escape from a bourgeois world or an avalanche of sequins.

Punishing the horn and rarely getting out of second gear, he went in surges among the mist-slowed traffic. He shot through a light just after it had turned red and was distantly discomforted to find himself sweeping across the junction in total safety. At the next traffic lights he arrived behind a furniture van.

Paint can in hand, Apple leapt out onto the roadway. He slammed the door closed with his foot while preparing the brush. The lights changed, the van moved away. Snapping his teeth, Apple got back in and followed.

On a straight run, going behind the same van at the same speed, unable to pass, he went across a series of junctions where the light was always green. He couldn't believe it. He kept shaking his head and giving incredulous smiles. But at last the van got stopped by a red.

Again Apple leapt out and slammed the door, taking no notice of the traffic beside him and behind him. He began to paint. He spread the black at speed over Ethel's glamour, dipping into the can frequently, standing in a spread-legged forward lean like a ping-pong player.

The van revved preparatory to leaving. There remained a square metre of Ethel still to be covered. Apple attacked it with a hissing industry that could have been more frenzied only if he were spreading water on a smouldering Monico.

The furniture van drove off with the green light. Apple went on painting like a lunatic. Traffic in the next lane went past with jeers and cheers, traffic behind began to clamour like a pack of robot foxhounds.

Apple told himself to finish the job later at the same time as he was telling himself there was no time like the present. He continued to slop and slap and spread. His arm kept on working even though his body was pulling away.

Mixed with the electronic yapping from behind were human cries. The first car's driver had his head through the window, showing a face as twisted and red as a knotted danger-flag.

The job was done. Apple waved assurances at the seething drivers as he followed the can inside. He drove off with the light hitting red, leaving the other cars to their honky racket.

Although Viceroy House was out of sight in the mist, Apple, who had three minutes in hand, knew by recognised buildings that he was close, therefore agreed with the idea that he ought to park before getting any closer. Except there were no spaces available along the packed kerbs.

Just as he was offering up the mental whine that he only needed to stop for a few minutes, Apple saw a gap between cars. It existed because not even a bumperless Mini could have been manoeuvred into it.

Apple swung the steering-wheel. With a snicker of rubber Ethel careened nose-first into the gap and bounced up the kerb. She came to a stop with her front wheels a metre or so on the pavement, causing two women carrying dogs to shy away in surprise and outrage.

Promising himself that it was okay, he had given the women something to talk about, an adventure (he was munificent today), Apple switched on the hire-sign light and got out. He knew the police would be apt to ignore this parking transgression, assume the taxicab to be involved in an emergency.

Which, Apple mused as he walked away, was obviously the kind of advantage he had been thinking of, on a lower, even more professional level, when he had first got the inspiration to paint Ethel black.

Apple was still nodding at this, with a shade of vehemence, and still not quite in sight of the apartment-hotel, when he saw Wendy.

He recognised her silhouette, which was showing in a car that stood parked some way ahead on this side. It was one of those plain, dark, impersonal cars that give themselves away as undercover transport by being so dark and impersonally plain. And Wendy was in it, here.

Apple had stopped walking. Although he had stopped nodding, physically, he went on doing so inside. He told himself that maybe a light had dawned.

Was a certain young lady's "sensitive" job that of an investigator?—he wondered. Had she been used by her bosses on account of being their only blusher? Had the enemy, suspecting her, tried to have her taken out of the picture? Was it because that hadn't worked, her getting free and later showing up at the meeting, that Blushers Anonymous had been closed down?

Smiling to show that he was intrigued, not at all irked, by the possibility of competition, Apple backed off.

When the dark car had been made hazy by the mist he stopped.

There was no need for him to check on the Barre Bentley, Apple knew. Wendy could see it from where she sat. She would follow it, obviously, and he would follow her.

Apple waited. For no other reason than to pass time, he assured himself, for certainly he wouldn't dream of interfering, he wasn't like that, no way, not at all, he mulled over ways in which the enemy, or someone, if they knew of Wendy's presence, could without violence render her inactive, at least in respect of her transportation.

They could let down one of her tyres. They could call the police, tell of the heroin dealer who sat here in a Ford Escort awaiting clients. They could siphon out all the petrol with a rubber tube. Masked, they could reach in her car and snatch the ignition keys. They could let down one of her tyres.

That one he had already had, Apple thought. Possibly because it was not only the simplest but the one with guaranteed success, as long as it was done on the farthest tyre from where she was sitting so she couldn't hear the hiss: police might not come or come too late, keys might not be gettable, petrol tank might be locked.

About to walk forward, Apple held at the sight of subdued action. Wendy, ending her watchful stillness, suddenly moved about; next, fumes came from the Escort's exhaust pipe. The procession looked to be getting ready for off.

Apple stepped further back into haziness. Not until the dark car, after reversing, began to pull out of its slot did he turn to run back.

Ethel was being ignored strenuously by passers-by, who could have been fearful of getting involved in whatever emergency it was that she seemed to represent. Congratulating himself on the brilliance of his planning, Apple got in.

He reversed quickly and with smooth style—and came to within four inches of a collision with a real taxi. The driver screamed above the wail of his brakes that Apple's unmarried parents had produced a carnally-conjoined subnormal who owned an old bathroom on wheels as aromatic as a practitioner of the oldest profession with a social malady.

Or so Apple translated into Greek as he switched off the hire sign and drove ahead, in order not to get riled by the insult to Ethel, who couldn't defend herself. Anger, he was aware, made not only for bad driving but inferior thinking all round.

The Escort was nicely some distance in front, with another car inbetween, over which both Ethel and Apple were tall enough to see with ease. They went by Viceroy House and Apple could only assume that the Bentley was somewhere ahead.

The procession went on. It led Apple along all the familiar roads, over the river and south-easterly.

From the door pocket at one stage Apple took a cap, which he put on and pulled low. It gave him an extra feeling of security, even though he was managing always to keep at least one vehicle between himself and the Escort.

Time passed. The mist stayed constant, the Bentley stayed unseen, Apple went on ignoring the people who hailed him with a curt "Taxi!" Whenever he found himself with no vehicle between Ethel and Wendy he dropped back, coming forward again with foglights on or hire sign lit to change the image.

It was when the procession had been half an hour on its way that the blob splattered onto the windshield. At first, his nostrils dilating, Apple thought it was a sparrow's gift, since he knew that such droppings were not white initially but colourless, just as the new-born babe is pale blue. He was repeating this fact mentally when the windshield was hit by two more large blobs.

"Rain," he said.

Glaring past the glass he examined the spread of new black. A fresh blob brought to about ten those that were already there, that when joined by others would wash the paint off, leaving Ethel in all her recognisable glory.

As Apple didn't believe in God, not having much time for the supernatural, he didn't put the blame on divine retribution (that shop-window vandalism), but decided that the fault could be placed at the muddy gumboots of Farmer Galling. His country neighbour was forever ranting at the skies to rain when it was fine and snarling at them to let up when it was raining, as if he felt he would be letting the farmer side down if he didn't act according to popular belief.

Apple remembered that what was possibly unique about Galling was his stated conviction that his rants and snarls actually worked. Apple knew this to be impossible, so when now he started to snarl with frequent, baleful glances upward he told himself he was only kidding, anything for a laugh; as well as, reminded by that recent translation, using a different language for every sentence of abuse; also keeping his mouth as still as possible and playing the radio so loudly that he couldn't hear himself.

He waited for the next blob. It didn't come. Tensely he went on with his insults, being inventive in a score of tongues and dissembling with the pretence that he was doing the normal neurotic's gambit of producing what he should have said to that taxi-driver. There were no more blobs.

Apple was back to radio and verbal peace, trauma

over, and already being missed, by the time he saw Wendy coming to a stop in the kerb. But it was only temporary. When she moved on again, Apple, who had hung back, saw a service station.

Lady Barre must have stopped there for petrol, he thought. Was she in for a long journey, perhaps crossing over to France? Would both the Escort and Ethel run out of fuel?

Humming, Apple drove on.

There was a series of roundabouts, those traffic islands which grow more frequent when the interminable suburbs are being slowly beaten, as, Apple allowed, they should be.

He had once more lost his intervening car to a side road as he came to another roundabout, this one in countryside. He stopped at the white line. The Escort was already circling at one side, and coming around at the other on a full circuit was a Bentley.

It, Apple saw with a twitch of alarm, belonged to Lady Barre. She sat there beside the driver, Jennifer Rolph. They both glanced without interest, an object for the eyes to rest on, at Apple, who, having shrunk, was additionally making a thorough job of scratching his eyebrow.

The big car passed and turned off at the next spoke. Along came the Escort. Wendy, features set, also sent Ethel and Apple a mechanical glance as she went curving past. She followed the Bentley at the same steady speed.

Not until the Escort had dissolved into the mist did Apple move off to tag on. Now that Ethel had been clearly seen, even in her pleasant plainness, he had to be extra cautious.

He went slowly along the spoke. The Escort he continued to keep out of sight. Only when he got overtaken by another car did he start to build up his pace. He failed to catch up to that other car. He went faster, and faster. The car stayed elusive, as though it had never been.

Apple put on more speed. He allowed the speedometer needle to climb in the way of which he didn't generally approve with Ethel, feeling that she ought to be treated with the respect to which her age entitled her.

Finally he saw the other car. This made him realise that it would undoubtedly have overtaken the Escort at the speed it was going, if Wendy hadn't already turned off. Either way, he knew he had come too far.

Apple brought Ethel to a shrieking stop. He made a fast turn, glad that a London taxi was the only vehicle extant that could circle in its own length, went surgingly back. His eyes on at glare, he watched for off-turnings.

On the left ahead, the fencing that bordered a ploughed field broke to give access to a lane. This could be it, Apple thought, but it could also not be. He hesitated, rubbed his nose, drove on.

There were trees, hedgerows, high weeps of willow. Next came a gravel track, again on the left. Apple took it because he felt he had gone far enough back.

Ethel speeded, bouncing as she went, between neatly clipped hedges and underneath tall trees with cathedral pretensions. Visibility was fifty feet.

A sign appeared, followed by two others. In turn they said, Private Road, Keep Out, Stonemason Manor.

Apple came to a gateway. The gate stood open. He went slowly through and then stopped. As he got out he insisted to himself that he was doing this for the simple reason that a gate on private property was always kept closed, and would certainly have been left so by the procession's leaders, meaning it must have been left open by impetuous Wendy, meaning that closed was its rightful position.

When, while swinging the gate across, being at a distance from the rumble of Ethel's motor, Apple heard ahead the sound of a car, he gave an I-told-you-so shrug to counter his knee-sag of relief.

He drove on. The gravel track climbed as it bore gradually to the right. It seemed to be circling an unsloping meadow that lay beyond the low hedge—a hedge whose increasing neatness suggested the proximity of Stonemason Manor.

Apple slowed. Ideally, he accepted, he ought to be approaching on foot. But there was no space for parking on the narrow track, which continued to make its easy-climbing sweep, and he wasn't about to start reversing.

There was a final section of curve and then the way changed, ending as it did so. It straightened, flattened and increased its width tenfold. It was the broad frontage to the house, itself dimly seen in the mist, with a row of fat cypress trees on either side.

In front of the house stood the Bentley—empty. The Escort Apple didn't see until, Ethel's tyres crunching gravel, he had slowly gone some way onto the frontage; then he saw the car's back, on the right between trees.

Copying, Apple took Ethel into Cypress cover, near the Escort. He switched the motor off, listened to the silence. Quietly he alighted. When he moved out onto the frontage, he met Wendy.

She was standing two metres away, by the rear of her car. Her arms were folded and her face was grim. She said, "I had a strange premonition it would be you."

Apple had stopped. He mumbled an awkward, unconvincing "Fancy seeing you here."

"I know, you're amazed."

"Well . . ."

"You've even got Ethel in disguise."

"I can explain that," Apple said.

Wendy said, "Don't bother. All I want you to do, Appleton, is go away as fast as you can. I don't know what you think you're playing at, but you can stop it."

"Who's playing?"

"I'll give you a call later. We'll have dinner."

"That's a nice idea."

"But now leave. Otherwise you'll be in danger of becoming a damn nuisance."

"Sorry about that."

"So—good-bye, Appleton."

"Nice place she has here," Apple said, looking past Wendy at the house. With a terrace two steps up from the gravel, it was a flat-faced, achingly bland building whose master would surely have turned away a Cavalier but given bread and water to a Roundhead. At one lower point light showed prettily in French windows opening onto the terrace.

Wendy asked, "Who has a nice place here?"

"Why, the lady of the manor."

"What d'you want with her?"

"Maybe the same thing you do."

They both alerted at a sound. It was the spaced crunch of footfalls on gravel. Open, not stealthy, the sound came from somewhere to Apple's rear. He looked over his shoulder, saw nothing, looked back at Wendy and asked, "Well?"

She asked, "Well what?"

The sound was growing. Apple turned again.

The man who came into view from out of the trees was medium build, averagely dressed, aged about forty, unremarkable save for the scar on one cheek.

He said a mild "Good afternoon."

Apple grunted. Wendy said nothing.

"I'm looking for the Wilkinson place," the man said. "I got confused in the mist."

Wendy asked a cool "Walking?"

"I left my car on the road."

"That's quite a trek."

"I shortcutted over the meadow from the gate," the man said easily. He looked at Apple. "How about the Wilkinsons?"

"I'm a stranger here," Apple said.

"Stay that way," Wendy told him. "Good-bye."

Looking around, Apple watched her walk off. When the man said that perhaps someone inside could help, he said, "I doubt it. I'd ask in the next village if I were you." He watched Wendy gain the terrace, stride to the French windows, open them without hesitation and go inside.

He turned, saying lightly, in a less-carrying tone, "Hi there, Bill."

The man said, "Hello, old son."

"Your hound technique is tops. Ten points. I never suspected I had a tail."

"You hadn't, so don't go losing sleep. I've been here five minutes, came straight here off my own bat."

"How?"

"Took a chance on it being where Lady Barre was headed."

"What gave you that idea in the first place, Bill?"

"Phone book. This is the Barre family manse."

"Oh," Apple said.

"Anyway, good to see you, old son."

"And you."

Upstairs had chosen to send Bill Burton, Apple was aware, because he was one of the few employees Apple knew by sight. Due to that memorable scar, Bill himself had never been used as an agent in the field. He played courier, driver and other peripheral rôles, or, if he got lucky, back-up man on someone else's caper.

Loving the casual pro-ness of all this, despite itching to go, get in the house, Apple asked, "You have a word for me?"

"Two," Bill Burton said. "Hot from the press. The first concerns a Jasper Pendleton."

"Which isn't his real name."

"Right. It's Fred Murphy."

"And he's a spook."

"Wrong. He's a fading confidence trickster. Obviously he got into this Blushers Anonymous lark thinking he'd find some soft touches—for bread, not brains."

"Well, he had the right idea."

Burton said, "So did lots of people. Within the last couple of days Blushers Anonymous has become big. Everyone's interested, the sheep as well as the wolves."

"Lady Barre cut off its head," Apple said, noting Bill's glibness, noting his own.

"Too many valuable sheep were joining or planning to join: Members of Parliament, Army people, a Second Secretary from the War Office."

After glancing back fretfully at the house Apple asked, "So MI5 stuck its nose in?"

"Special Branch," Bill Burton said. "Lady Barre checked out as clean, but there were too many fat sheep laying themselves open to approach, so the Branch asked her nicely, it says in small print, to close down Blushers Anonymous in the name of national security."

"Lady Barre's clean?"

"According to the Branch. Of whom it's said in some quarters that it's always the last to twig."

"Mmm," Apple said.

Bill Burton jerked an elbow aside, asking, "That old taxi wouldn't be . . . ?"

"She would. If I had the time I'd tell you about the problem I had with her log-book."

"Heard it. Gossip says God gave you a new one because the first, being a fake, put him onto a mole who's been safely retired for years."

"And there I was, thinking old Angus had turned human."

"That'll be the day."

Apple asked, "But what about my second word?"

"Yes, Pewter Farm. It was rented by a certain Miriam Kean. That do you any good?"

"No. Meaningless."

"Thought it might be," Bill Burton said. "People do play naughty games with names. But there's a description that might help. You want it?"

"Like a kid wants Christmas."

"So listen."

Apple listened. He would have started to smile if he hadn't been in Bill's company. He didn't want to slip to the amateur, be un-pro, especially after he had been coming up with such snappy bits of dialogue.

He said a blasé, "Thanks, Bill."

"My pleasure, old son."

"If there's nothing else . . ."

"That's the lot," Bill Burton said. "So I'll now fade mysteriously into the mist—unless you want help." Behind his droll style, as all along, there lay a plaintive element, the understudy to healthy stars, the jockey grown fat.

Hurriedly, before his melting sensation could intensify, Apple turned away. "Fade on, Bill," he said with a cool salute. "See you around."

From a distance of several feet, not wishing to be seen, Apple looked through the French windows at the room they served. On the whole, he approved.

Where there should have been pictures, there were footprints. Where a chandelier ought to have been hanging, there was a wooden slab in the form of a mattress, with light bulbs in place of buttons. Where you would expect to see books in a bookcase, there were numerous bowls of tropical fish. The skeleton lying in a hammock that transversed a far corner was wearing soccer boots.

Seating was a disappointment: the pair of armchairs and the long couch they faced were out of page one thousand in a mail-order catalogue. Saving the ensemble, however, was the separating piece of furniture, a junior-size billiard table brought to its knees by a saw.

Wendy, sitting in an armchair, had her back to the windows. Lady Barre and Jennifer Rolph were facing her on the couch, latter sitting up erect and serious, former sprawled back with a light smile, the essence of superiority in purple overalls.

Apple stepped closer, tapped politely on the glass and then went inside. Jennifer and Lady Barre perked, Wendy twisted around. Although using a different timbre for their words, each woman said the same thing: "Well well."

"Good afternoon, ladies," Apple said, affable. He closed the French window. "I do hope you'll forgive my intrusion."

Wendy said, "Some might." Her voice was as soft as a life sentence.

"Does it strike you that front doors seem to have gone out of fashion?" Lady Barre asked of Jennifer Rolph, who answered, "Vividly."

Apple went to the hearth on his left, where a coal fire burned as soothingly as a smile to the doubtful. "In my case, ma'am, I thought I'd save your servants the trouble."

Lady Barre gave an amused snort. "My servants are called Mrs. Jenkins and she wouldn't dream of leaving her kitchen to open the door for anyone." She waved a regal hand. "But let's get to you, young Appleton."

"Let's."

"This is quite a surprise."

Cheerfully: "I suppose it is."

"Wendy we expected to roll up, as we've been telling her, haven't we, dear?"

Wendy nodded, face inscrutable, and Apple asked, "Oh?"

"We kept seeing the same car behind us, so we took a full turn of the last roundabout and saw who it was."

"I was trying to catch up," Wendy said indifferently, which she dropped on looking at Apple with "I thought you were going."

"Changed my mind."

"That was foolish of you."

Still warming his back by the fire, Apple said, "It would've been ill-mannered to leave without stopping in to say hello."

Lady Barre, who was nearest on the couch, folded her arms. "This is all very odd, of course. Funny peculiar. Wouldn't you agree, Jen?"

Jennifer Rolph said a short, efficient "Entirely."

"But fascinating."

"Oh yes. Most."

"Perhaps, Appleton, you are connected with those gentlemen who came to see me yesterday."

"I? No. I'm not connected with anybody."

Lady Barre said, "That's what Wendy here was just telling us about herself, so presumably that means you two are not in league."

"It does."

Wendy: "I don't know which gentlemen you mean, anyway."

"Doesn't matter, dear," Lady Barre said. "Possibly, then, you came to see about keeping my brain-child afloat."

"I'm afraid not."

Lady Barre looked at Apple. "Are you interested in keeping Blushers Anonymous alive, Appleton?"

"At this moment in time," Apple said like a politician, "I'm unable to oblige."

"But you do believe in its viability, I feel sure."

"One hundred per cent."

"And you, Wendy dear?"

"Two hundred per cent. A lovely idea."

Unfolding her arms, clasping her hands, Lady Barre said, "Fine. But suppose we now get down to cases. Or rather, to one single case. That one there." She nodded a direction.

At Wendy's end of the flotsam-covered billiard table, five feet from where she sat, was the red pigskin bag, with its mate stood up toward the other end.

"Our Files, in point," Lady Barre said. "You told us you'd like to have them, Wendy."

"That's right."

"But if you don't intend trying to carry on with Blushers Anonymous, what would you do with them?"

Looking relaxed, confident, tough, Wendy said, "I'd rather not go into that, if you'll pardon my reticence."

"I'll pardon anything, dear, as long as it's something I've done myself."

Apple asked, "Weren't those aforementioned gentlemen interested in the Files?"

Jennifer Rolph answered. She said, "The Files weren't brought up. The men probably don't know about them."

Lady Barre said, "I can't understand why they've suddenly become so important."

"I can tell you that," Apple said. He knew he would have to do some hand-forcing, for he had no intentions of blowing his cover. "I know why."

"Then pray tell, young Appleton."

"The reason I know is because of a very strange experience I had today. I won't bore you with details, the danger and so forth, but after that I talked to a friend of mine who used to be with the police."

"Scotland Yard?" Lady Barre asked. "Special Branch?"

"Nothing so grand," Apple said. "Retired now, Jim was a detective-sergeant with the Bloomsbury division. And look, Jim told me that obviously there was some jiggery-pokery going on. He'll be sending a memo to a high-up about it."

"Delightful phrase," Lady Barre murmured with sensuous eyes. "Jiggery-pokery."

"Jim pointed out to me that if the Files fell into unscrupulous hands, the people on file could suffer."

Jennifer asked, "Unscrupulous?"

"Criminal, that is," Apple said, since a philologist and a detective-sergeant would hardly suspect a foreign hand in the matter. "Extortionists, blackmailers, swindlers. To these types your Files represent a little gold mine."

"Sounds marvellous," Lady Barre said. "I'm not sure, however, that I understand."

"These types prey on the sensitive and the insecure."

"Blushers, in fact."

"Right. Members of BA, people on file, could be relieved of cash in various ways, generally put through the wringer."

"I see. Yes, I do see."

"It wouldn't surprise me at all to learn that among the members is a confidence trickster or two."

"Marvellous. Terrible too, of course."

Apple said, "The reason I came here, ma'am, came so unorthodoxly, was to suggest that the Files be destroyed. They could fall into the wrong hands."

Lady Barre nodded. "That's fine with me."

"So why don't we do it now?"

"Again, Appleton, that's fine with me."

"This fire'll do the job perfectly," Apple said. He strode to the table, lifted the red case.

"No," Jennifer Rolph said.

Apple: "I beg your pardon?"

"Sorry."

Lady Barre asked, "What is it, dear?"

"Don't mind me," Jennifer said. "Just being selfish."

"Selfish, Jen?"

"When I think of the hours of labour I put in on that data. Making notes and then typing them out."

"You've been absolutely dedicated, dear."

"I loved it. I considered it eminently worthwhile work. I still do."

Lady Barre said, "But if the Files pose a threat to innocent people . . ."

"Quite so," Jennifer Rolph said. "Of course they must be destroyed." She gestured. "Please continue, Appleton. I'm sorry for interrupting."

As Apple turned away, Wendy spoke. She said, "That's far enough." He turned back and saw that she was holding a gun. He remembered to look surprised.

After a long silence Lady Barre asked, "Is that gun real?" Her tone held more hope than worry.

"Real and loaded," Wendy said blithely.

Looking down at her, Apple said, "I don't believe you'd really use it."

"Be healthier if you did, Appleton. I wouldn't kill anyone, no, the prize here isn't worth it, but a bullet in the right place can be pretty messy."

"That I believe."

"Put the case back."

After he had obeyed meekly Apple used the table for himself, sitting on its end facing Wendy with a covering lie or two: "I never had a gun pointed at me before. I've gone weak in the knees."

Jennifer: "I feel weakish myself, Appleton."

"So," Lady Barre said following a brisk clap of the hands. "So it turns out that you are actually a *criminal,* Wendy dear. How terribly exciting."

"Criminal nothing," Wendy said with a tinge of hauteur. "Crime is decadence."

"Be that as it may, I can't imagine that you're doing this for fun."

"The people I represent have high aims."

"High aims, eh? Not sure that I know what you mean by that. What does she mean, Appleton?"

Apple shrugged and Jennifer said, "Political."

Wendy nodded. "I dare say that's the word."

Putting her hands together again Lady Barre pointed them as though they held a gun in that manner touted in visual fiction as orthodox but rarely used when the bullets were flying.

She said, "Please don't tell me you're one of those dreary Labour people."

Jennifer Rolph said, "I don't think, Lady Barre, that Labourites go around threatening people with guns."

"You never know what the bloody Socialists get up to. And that, I see now, I really do see now, is it. They could approach these innocent, sensitive types in our Files and *brainwash* 'em."

Wendy: "For what?"

"Into thinking Leftly."

Wendy unreeled a toneless, "Brainwashing is an invention of the West."

While this exchange had been going on, Apple, finished congratulating himself on being nearly right in respect of Blushers Anonymous, had settled on what approach to use in order to have all the facts. Not that they were important, except as dressing for when he mentioned his triumph to Angus Watkin.

The best way to get someone to tell the truth, Apple recalled from Training Five, in addition to using flattery and insult, was to lie. To lie, that is, when saying you knew the score. Lie to put the subject on the defensive, want to improve his image or be protective of himself. Example: to have a man admit he had stolen a car, you said you knew he had committed murder.

In a similar vein, when it wasn't a matter of confession but merely to discover method or earn confirmation, you suggested knowledge with a superior smile so as to give the subject the chance to top you, feel smart.

That the routine might work with Wendy had been established by her having been disinclined to have herself classed as a common criminal.

As far as the Files were concerned, Apple had decided how to handle that element the moment he had seen the red case which now stood immediately behind him.

Lady Barre was saying that she didn't know what to think. Apple, blinking innocently, said, "Wait a minute. *Decadence.* The *West.* The answer's there somewhere."

Not without a hint of fondness, Wendy said, "Who's my clever Appleton, then?"

Still blinking: "That sounds like sarcasm."

"I must be on my way."

"Wait," Apple said. "I think I've got it. I believe I've got you placed."

"Go on."

"You, Wendy, are from behind the Iron Curtain."

She smiled. "Something like that."

"And you're a *spy,*" Apple said, making himself look impressed.

"Political investigator is the term I prefer."

"Oh, I say," Lady Barre said. "How exciting. An agent in the cloak and dagger world."

Wendy told Apple, "It's what I thought you were. One of the counter variety."

Apple leaned back as though with delighted surprise, which he subdued because he felt he might be overdoing it the moment his elbow had touched, and moved backwards several inches, the red case.

He asked, "You thought I was a spy?"

"For a time."

While Jennifer, behind him on his left, was explaining to her employer that an unfriendly power would no doubt find useful sensitive people who had important jobs, of whom there were many in the Files, Apple was telling Wendy that he began to see it all now, it was as clear as day.

"Your bosses heard that the CIA or somebody was finding Blushers Anonymous interesting and so they got in on the act."

"It was my own idea, actually."

"And then you thought I was onto your game."

"I soon changed my mind. You were too sweet, too normal. The cottage, Monico, the Ethel business. And your spouting of anti-Communist rubbish at the party was too corny to be a performance."

"So why did you shove me off the balcony?"

Lady Barre asked, "What's that?"

As Apple turned to her to explain while Wendy was saying because his talk had angered her, he managed to push the red case another few inches along the table.

Facing Wendy again Apple said, "Somebody else must have thought I was on to them as well, the same people who kidnapped you, going by method, because today . . . but there's no need to go into all that."

"The strange experience you mentioned earlier?"

"That's right."

Wendy smiled amiably. "You must mean your flight abroad."

Once more Apple did his blinks. "You know?"

"Of course. We arranged it."

"The blanket with ether, the imitation helicopter?"

"A neat idea, wouldn't you agree?"

"Brilliant."

"Thank you," Wendy said.

"I suppose your bosses own that place," Apple said on account of he couldn't say he knew that Wendy, as Miriam Kean, had organised the rental. Nor would he bring up what he now realised: Wendy had not been aware of the extensive Files until he himself had told her about them, in Harlequin Mansions, when he had explained about being caught looking into them by Lady Barre; that Wendy had not been able to do anything about it that night because she couldn't get out, he having secret-locked the apartment door; that she had embarked on the tailing of the Barre Bentley after having received the same information he had got, from Viceroy House's receptionist.

Wendy asked, "How did you come up with that neat idea of escaping, Appleton?"

"I'll tell you if you tell me about the kidnapping, why you did it. You said you'd stopped thinking I was a counter-spy."

"But there might, after all, have been something in you as a scientist. Is there?"

"Only to another philologist."

"Okay. Your escape."

Apple lied, "I got the ladder idea from an espionage novel. It's my favourite type of reading."

"Lovely," Lady Barre said. "Me too. After romances. Do you like E. Phillips Oppenheim?"

"Very much."

"I've got all his books, which I'll loan you if you promise, promise most faithfully, to bring them back."

Apple, over his shoulder: "I'm meticulous in that respect, Lady Barre."

"Good man. But what was that about an escape?"

"I'll explain later."

"Yes, when I've gone," Wendy said, making to rise. She stopped when Apple spoke.

"Kidnapping me was easily arranged," he said, adding what he knew to be impossible, "You simply followed me to the ALTOG examination and back."

"Nothing so boring," Wendy said. "We were in the garage ready and waiting when you returned."

"So you had a nice long wait."

"Not at all. The note you left for me not only explained all about the ALTOG deal, it even gave the expected return time. You're very obliging, Appleton."

Ignoring that completely he said, "We? That must refer to the imitation landlady."

"An efficient colleague."

"She hit me, I now realise, for the same reason you pushed me off the balcony. I must've made some anti-Communist crack without thinking."

"Nothing of the sort. She's quite liberal. Having seen me snatched, she wanted to read the room and see who the baddies were. Nationality."

Apple, knowing: "Read the room?"

"Forget it," Wendy said. "But you were just about to spoil things by tidying up."

"Talking of hits," Apple said. "You must have belted me on the back of the head in that alley." He laughed. "No, what's wrong with me. That was too well done to be a woman's job. I got mugged, that's all. I'm beginning to see you as Superwoman."

During this, Apple, reaching behind as though leaning, shoved the red case a foot back, stopping when both Lady Barre and Jennifer made coughing sounds with a warning flavour, like patients when the ward nurse comes in.

Casually, Wendy said yes, she had knocked him out to check his credentials. "You think I'm not hard enough? Listen, I know the ropes. I disabled two Israeli agents to get out of that house they took me to."

"So it was true, your story, or nearly so," Apple said, glad he had been right there. He showed a bemused expression. "I think I'm in over my head."

"I'll say you are."

"But I came in handy for you, didn't I? My flat was a useful refuge from those other spies."

"Yes, Appleton. I must thank you for your hospitality."

Lady Barre asked Jennifer if she knew what they were talking about and Jennifer said she didn't. Apple asked Wendy what the Israelis had wanted.

"To find out what was happening with Blushers Anonymous, of course. They hadn't managed to put one of their own people in yet."

"I suppose they didn't have a blusher," Apple said. "In fact, I suppose that's the reason your bosses used you in this thing. You blush."

"No, I don't," Wendy said. "I don't blush at all."

"But you hid behind the curtain."

"That was so no one could see I wasn't blushing."

"I say, that was rather ingenious of you, dear," Lady Barre said, which cued Apple into sagging back as though with admiration, which enabled him to give another shove to the red case, which brought from Jennifer more coughing.

But Wendy hadn't noticed, Apple knew. He also knew he could not expect to keep her talking much longer. As it was, he had done marvellously, and it was tragic that Angus Watkin would hear about all this only at second hand and wouldn't believe a word.

"What's the next move, Wendy?" Apple asked.

"To go peacefully upon my way, Appleton."

"And after that?"

"None of your business," Wendy said without rancour. She began to get up from the deep armchair, swaying forward. "If you would be kind enough to pass me that bag with the Files."

It was the classic moment for the man under the gun to make his move, jump the gun person. Even if it were necessary, however, even vital, Apple doubted if he could bring himself to risk the consequences. Death he didn't mind, as he wouldn't be around afterwards to regret its having happened; disabling he could do without.

Getting up to a crouch, Apple turned. The Files case was near its red mate. With a swift, sure movement, his body playing shield, Apple reached along the dwarf billiard table and lifted the innocuous of the two cases.

Lady Barre got up fast with a sudden burst of talk and Jennifer gave one booming cough. Grateful for their attempts at diverting Wendy's attention, Apple turned, straightening.

Lady Barre fell silent as Wendy, standing, looked from one to the other of the three. She asked, "Something wrong?"

Apple said, "Perhaps you would like to reconsider."

"Change my ideology?"

"You needn't go that far. Just let the Files stay here so they can be destroyed."

"Sorry, Appleton," Wendy said. "Now put the bag down on the floor in front of you, and then, with arms out at the sides, move back to the other side of the couch, by the wall."

Wearing an expression of regret, which he thought quite well done, Apple followed orders. On turning by the wall he saw that Wendy had lifted the case.

Lady Barre told her, "It's not too late to change your mind, you know, dear."

Wendy answered with a wink. Moving semi-sideways she circled her armchair and went to the French window, which she opened with an elbow.

"That's all, ladies and gentleman," she said, saluting with the gun. "Thank you and good-bye." She slipped out.

Lady Barre sat down with a flop. Apple, humming lightly, strolled around to the window and closed it neatly. He was debating if he should look at his finger-nails when Lady Barre said, "What a shame."

Apple faced the couch warily. "What?" he said with a protective smile, and then said it again with a facial droop after Jennifer had told him that Wendy was in possession of the Files.

"We did try to warn you," Lady Barre said apologetically. "Every time you worked on switching the two cases we coughed at you and things."

Apple asked his third "What?"

Jennifer explained, her manner sympathetic, "You see, Appleton, I had already switched the cases just before you came in, I'm afraid."

"And rather brilliantly," Lady Barre said. "I must give you my sincere congratulations, dear."

"Thank you."

As Apple, showing the smile of a soldier who is picked to volunteer, lied in untidy mumbles that he had sort of suspected his adroit ruse of being possibly in error, both women lowered their eyes, as though out of common decency.

Apple said, "But I had to take the chance."

"Of *course,*" they said in warm unison. Jennifer added, "You mustn't blame yourself for a moment."

"Absolutely not," Lady Barre said stoutly. "And let's face it, we've been bested by a real true professional. It's nothing to be ashamed of."

Jennifer nodded. "I have an idea Wendy may have seen my switch and then seen yours. We're not in the lady's league at these games."

Stung, Apple stood tall. He said, said as from beyond the glass he heard a car start, "Oh, we're not, eh?"

Lady Barre: "You mustn't feel hurt, young Appleton."

"We'll see about leagues."

Jennifer sat forward. "What're you going to do?"

Apple opened the French window. "To be quite honest, I have no idea yet."

"Be careful. Don't forget she has a gun."

"Hold the fort," Apple said while slipping outside, where he was in time to see, mistily, the Escort reversing this way from between the trees. He closed the window. By the time the car started forward, he had made his weak plan and was running along the terrace.

Leaping down to the gravel Apple set off crunchingly toward the cypress trees. At this point it was merely a half-dozen strides, but the gravel's mud-like lack of resistance made each footfall an effort, which is why he had decided against heading for Ethel.

Apple knew, in any case, that even if he got to Ethel quickly he would be unable to overtake on the narrow track; and out on the highway the Escort would leave him dawdling.

As for the Bentley, at hand, if he did manage to get the keys nimbly, it also would be left behind by Wendy's car, since the only fast needle in Bentleys and their Rolls Royce twins was on the fuel gauge.

Behind the trees Apple came to a low, ornamental wall. Beyond it lay the meadow which sloped down to the gate and around, which the Escort had to travel.

Apple cleared the wall in a jump. His manner was wild even though he knew that his chances of getting to the gate before Wendy were dismal. Nerves and pique and bravado more than hope of success kept him on the way, sent him now racing headlong down the mist-wrapped meadow.

But then hope came alive in him as he heard Wendy's car come to a stop. He thought it could have broken down until, next, came a gunshot.

Apple went on running. He waited. He nodded when another gunshot sounded. A moment later he heard the Escort move on again.

That pause, Apple reckoned, had been worth a good twenty seconds. Its purpose, obviously, was for Wendy to do what was right and proper for wise agents to do: disable any vehicle that could be used to give chase. In this case it meant shooting out one of Ethel's tyres and one on the Bentley.

Apple ran. The downslope going helped, as did, more so, his new-found hope, for he knew that nothing aided winners more than their conviction that they were going to win.

With the fragile wall of mist keeping its flirty distance, Apple charged on. He was conscious of the car humming somewhere over to his right and reminding himself that tyres were no more an intrinsic part of a vehicle than clothing was of a person.

Therefore Ethel had not been wounded, Apple repeated to himself, which truth kept him from confronting like a man the fact that he loved the notion of Ethel receiving a wound in the line of duty.

Apple tripped. His foot, in landing, had hit a hummock of grass toe-on. Over he went into a dive, his limbs as graceful as on a swastika. He was glad no one could see.

Landing on his hands expertly, he formed himself into a ball and encouraged the ball to roll. It was all smooth and professional and painless. The grass was soaking wet. When his rolling had stopped he got up sodden down the back from hair to socks.

Showing his bottom teeth because it was all part of the spy game, like being hurled from high balconies, brutally attacked in alleys and bed-sitters and garages, chased by undercover policemen along city streets and locked in bleak cells, Apple raced on. He declined to reckon that by falling he had forfeited three seconds.

Just as the Escort's hum was growing depressingly loud, Apple saw trees. But they were not part of his goal, those that sided the lane; they merely formed a copse in the meadow. Apple frowned at them as he charged through.

Instantly, on clearing the copse, he saw the hedge. It appeared cheerily through the mist. The high trees paced along in either direction and centrally stood the gate, which was as it had been left, closed, allowing Apple to forget his wet back by acknowledging his astuteness in planning ahead.

His new headlong dive, as the car's noise swooped higher, was intentional. From his soggy landing he rolled obliquely, aimed for Wendy's side of the gate. He had just reached hidingly the hedge's lee when the noise became fully clear, meaning its maker had come out of the sound-muting mist.

Next, peering through foliage from his crouch, Apple saw the Escort go by, slowing rapidly as it did. Wendy had her jaw out like a heroine. She braked when ten feet back from the gate to allow for opening.

Apple had already pulled his shoes off by the time Wendy had set the hand-brake, put the drive in neutral and opened the door. She threw quick ferrety glances all around as she alighted, more during her walk to the gate. She bent to the latch.

Fast as four words, Apple jumped the metre-high hedge, which was as nothing to a man of his stature. In landing on the gravel he made no sound, being shoeless —as well as ruthless in gagging back his yell of pain at the stab of gravel on his soles.

The latch came up with a click. Wendy began to trudge the heavy gate open, coming backwards.

Apple, mouth closed, pained his way at delicate speed to the car's wide-open door. Quiet though he was, he knew Wendy would have heard him if it hadn't been for her own crunching.

The red case, when Apple looked in the Escort, wasn't to be seen. He looked in the back. It was there, on the floor. He stooped inside above the driver's seat and with an arm of whose length he had never been so fond reached the case. Grasping its handle he lifted and withdrew.

Wendy dropped the gate. As she turned, Apple sank down behind the door; as she started her return, he squat-walked to the rear and around the back, his mouth in an obscene curl at the agony of his soles.

Wendy reached the car, got in, slammed the door. It was while she was busying herself with drive and brake that Apple rose, took one step and then leapt over the hedge. On the grass he at once shot flat and scrumpled back close to the hedgerow.

The Escort drove on. Within seconds the sound of its motor had faded. Apple was beginning to put on his shoes when he heard the voice. It said, "Well done."

The cool pro, Apple went on tying laces as he glanced up and behind. Looking over the hedge at him was Bill Burton, his face displaying a smile. Apple didn't know if it was the angle of vision, or if there was a true element in that smile of something he didn't like.

He asked, after offering thanks for the compliment, "You playing back-up, Bill?"

"Well, not so much playing, old son. God asked me to keep an eye open."

"Ah, I see."

"Must be wet, sitting there."

"Somewhat," Apple said. He finished one shoelace and started on the other.

Bill Burton said, "I'm a bit surprised to see you, matter of fact."

"Why's that?"

"I heard a shot. Two, to be precise. I thought maybe you'd bought it, gone to that Great Big Trenchcoat in the Sky."

"The lady shot out tyres. The Bentley and Ethel."

"Gallant old Eth," Bill Burton said. "I didn't expect to see you'd changed her finery for the black. Too bad."

"Temporary only, Bill. It was a disguise for tailing."

"Clever, I'd say."

"Later today I'll clean the black paint off," Apple said. He smiled. He was pleased at his decision despite the fact that he was telling himself he had known all along he wouldn't really go through with the Antique London

Taxicab Owners Guild nonsense, give in to the demands of snobbery.

Bill Burton said, "Ethel looks happier dressed up."

"You're right," Apple said. "And talking of drab cars, I wonder if you happened to notice that Escort's headlights."

"One glass was yellowy—that what you mean?"

"Yes. Thanks. Pieces in puzzles. You know."

"Sure. From hearsay."

Shoelace tied, Apple got up. His bottom was cold and wet. Stooping, he lifted the red case, whereupon Bill Burton asked, "That has the BA Files?"

"How do you know about 'em?"

"Me, I don't know about anything, old son. But God knows."

"Yes, naturally."

"They're what he asked me to keep an eye open for," Bill Burton said.

"I might've known it wouldn't be for me."

"And he told me to collect them, if poss."

Apple said, "I was going to chuck 'em in the fire."

"Old Angus probably thought you might have something like that in mind," Bill Burton said. "Hence my orders."

"What's he going to do with the data?"

"Search me."

"I could say the same. But we know, of course."

"Sure we do."

Apple said, "It doesn't matter that these people are Brits. They're sensitive, therefore a soft touch, therefore usable in one way or another. That they might get hurt is immaterial."

Proffering a flat hand as though to support an apology, Bill Burton said, "Angus Watkin is a top spook. He'd use his mother if it would help. That's his job."

Apple shook the case. "What we could do is make a fire right here with these papers. If I don't dry myself quickly I might catch pneumonia. That's the story."

"Sorry, old son," Bill said. He still had his hand out. "God has his job, I have mine."

"The story's not without a wink of truth."

"Sorry."

After a sharp sigh like a mute's snarl, Apple reached across the hedge and gave the case to his colleague, who said, "Don't blame me."

"I don't, Bill."

They shook their heads at one another. The scar-faced man asked, "Want a hand with that spare tyre?"

"No, thanks," Apple said. "Anyway, I'll go in the house first, have a cuppa tea and a wrap-up chat with the ladies. La Barre and the girl with green eyes."

"You've had fun."

"It's had its moments." He turned away. "See you, Bill."

"Take care, old son."

Apple strode off toward the copse, climbing gently. He reminded himself that it was always possible for Watkin's intentions to be innocent; for him to plan on destroying the Files and want to see this happen personally.

But Apple knew he was being naïve. Angus Watkin wouldn't dream of wasting a list of potential tools. At the least, during dull times in the spy game he could practice entrapment.

"Hold it!"

Apple, who had just entered the copse, jerked to a halt at the command. He would have been less surprised if the voice had been male.

"Lift both arms at the sides."

Apple raised his arms, slowly. He still hadn't got them

fully up level with his shoulders, his mind playing with
the woman's voice, when she ordered, "Turn around."
   He turned.
   There was no one there.
   He could see nothing but mist beyond the nearest
tree.
   Then Apple realised that the orders were not for himself. They were for Bill Burton. He further realised that
the voice belonged to the woman who had played landlady and who had made the phony telephone call at
Pewter Farm.
   Apple crept forward swiftly, keeping behind a tree.
Within six steps he could see, beyond the hedge, the
upper parts of two human forms.
   The nearest and clearest was Bill Burton, his back
turned, his arms raised like a boy playing airplane, one
hand holding the red case. Just coming to a stop in front
of him, less clear, was Witch-face. Her gun she held in a
manner that told of familiarity.
   Apple was amused. Next to being destroyed or hidden
or otherwise rendered unavailable, the best fate for the
Files was to go to the other side. If they were held by
Upstairs, it would be disloyal to interfere, but that could
be done to make them comparatively tame in the possession of Wendy & Co.: with help from Jennifer's memory,
all Blushers Anonymous members could be contacted
and warned.
   While he had been thinking, Apple saw, the case had
changed ownership. Lovely, he thought. And it was
surely no skin off *his* nose. He had pulled off this little
caper with total success. He was golden.
   Carrying the red case, her face again making that mistake of smiling, the woman began to back away.
   A voice insulted the silence. In Russian, it ordered a
harsh "Halt right there!"

Witch-face stopped short as though tugged, Bill Burton jerked his raised arms, Apple twitched with nerves and wished he had the common sense to warn himself when he was going to do these odd things.

Still speaking in Russian, still disguising his voice with harshness, Apple called out, "You are covered from three sides. Understand?"

Her features straight ugly, the woman gave one heavy nod.

"Drop the case," Apple commanded, adding to his tone a measure of contempt. "Drop the gun."

While the woman obeyed, reluctantly, one object at a time, gun first, Apple was starting to understand his action. It was not simply a matter of saving Bill Burton from Angus Watkin's wrath. It was also, in greater degree, Bill himself. Rarely had he been involved in an operation so closely. This was rich for him—and it had been about to end in shabbiness, failure.

"Get going down the lane," Apple ordered. "Fast."

After taking two steps backwards, her face more of a match than ever for broomsticks and tall hats, the woman paused.

"Fast, I said!" Apple shouted. He crossed his fingers and then snappingly uncrossed them because it was ridiculous.

Witch-face swung around. She ran to the gateway, passed through it and went quickly on. Her form dissolved, her footfalls grew faint.

Hesitantly, Bill Burton picked up the case and the gun. His turn was slow. Peering all around, with repeat looks toward the copse, he asked in a near whisper, asked with uncertainty, "Is that you, old son?"

Apple reversed from the tree quietly.

"Apple?" Bill asked. "Is it you?"

When his colleague's form was beginning to fade in haziness, Apple turned away. Smiling, he went off into the mist.

ABOUT THE AUTHOR

Marc Lovell is the author of ten previous Appleton Porter novels, including *The Spy Who Barked in the Night* and *The Spy Who Got His Feet Wet*. *Apple Spy in the Sky* was made into the film *Trouble at the Royal Rose*. Mr. Lovell has lived for over twenty years on the island of Majorca.